POTPOURRI

Ruskin Bond

Rupa . Co

Published 2007 by
Rupa . Co
7/16, Ansari Road, Daryaganj,
New Delhi 110 002

Sales Centres:

Allahabad Bangalore Chandigarh
Chennai Hyderabad Jaipur Kathmandu
Kolkata Mumbai Pune

Typeset in 13 pt. AmericanGaramond
Mindways Design
1410 Chiranjiv Tower,
43 Nehru Place
New Delhi 110 019

Printed in India by
Saurabh Printers Pvt. Ltd.
A-16, Sector-IV,
Noida 201 301

Contents

Introduction

A question that always irritates me is, 'And are you still writing?'

It's like asking me if I'm still alive, because if I wasn't writing I wouldn't be alive—I'd have become a vegetable, mentally deficient, or sunk far below the poverty line. Indeed, I would also be spiritually dead, because words are my life-blood. I mean the written word. My spoken words are few. My written words are many; and sometimes true.

I am writing this page while the walls of my room are being repaired. There is loud hammering and the sound of falling plaster. Dust everywhere. The room's a mess. Very irritating. But that doesn't stop me from writing. A compulsive writer will write anywhere—on a train or platform bench, in a noisy hotel lounge, wayside teashop, or school playground.

Here comes Vaishnavi's rubber ball. Vaishnavi is two and a half, at home while her older brothers and sisters are at school. She wants me to play with her. I say later. She throws the ball at me, and it just misses my coffee cup. Her mother picks her up and takes her into the kitchen, where she is quite happy counting spoons. I carry on writing.

Those young readers who have given me pens are the wise ones. They know I'm still writing—and that I'm still using a pen, albeit a ball-point or roller-ball. I'm a clumsy fellow and draw the line at fountain-pens, as inevitably I get ink all over my fingers and shirt-sleeves. So you could say I've kept up with the times. After all, Mr Amitabh Bachchan, movie star, recommends a certain elegant ball-point pen, and that's the one I'm usually given.

I'm an old-fashioned person. Even as a boy I was old-fashioned. I liked old music, old books, old films, old places. I still do.... In fact, I'm so old-fashioned and out of date that it's a wonder I've survived for over seventy years.

I can't drive, preferring to put my faith in the driving abilities of my friends and companions. The worst of drivers find me the perfect passenger, as I haven't the slightest idea if he's putting us at risk or not. In fact, I judge a driver by the amount of abuse he gets from other drivers. If, in the course of a day's journey, his sister or mother is insulted on at least six occasions, then I begin to suspect that there is something wrong with the way he drives. If he returns the insults tenfold, I ask him to stop, and get off before we are assaulted.

I can row a boat at India Gate or the Model Town lake, but I can't fly a plane. When I was five, one of the Jamnagar princes took me and my mother up in a Tiger Moth, one of those four-winged contraptions that are open to the sky. I was terrified, especially when he decided to indulge in some aerial acrobatics. I was sick all over him, I'm glad to say.

For the next fifty years I avoided aeroplanes, preferring to travel by train, camel or mule—there's nothing like sitting on a mule to stiffen to sinews and summon up the blood, as the bard would say—and even today it is with great reluctance that I trust myself to the airways. Others of my age don't seem to be bothered by the incipient hazards of flight. A lady sitting next to me was engrossed in an Agatha Christie novel, *Death in the Air*, while on another flight my companion, a young publisher, was reading the manuscript of a book about the hijacking of a plane that had been on the very same route as ours.

There's no place like home, even if I do happen to be living in an earthquake zone.

I think the hardest thing in life is dealing with failure—putting it behind and carrying on with what you're doing and trying to do it well.

When I look back over the years, and think of the books that never took off, the long years of little or no recognition or reward, I'm surprised that I did not throw it all up and turn to something else—something boring but safe.

I'm not one for taking risks, but I took one great risk—the risk of my life—and stuck to what I knew I could do well and what I wanted to do most. And with that came a measure of happiness. And in that happy frame of mind I could deal with all the little failures that came my way. I did not really see them as failures but rather as road-blocks. You do not retreat from a road-block; you make your way around it, or look for another route to where you are going.

And you learn to zigzag ... Take a different route, albeit a longer one. Try something different. If the novel fails, write a a story for children. If no one wants your poetry, write a prose-poem. Go back to writing for yourself. If you can't be a Dickens, be a Lamb. There's room in the world for all kinds of writers, all kinds of talents. Be different. Use your own voice. It will take a little longer for readers to get used to your own unique voice, but when they do, they will want more of it.

There are no fresh starts in life, but there are always new directions.

Ruskin Bond
July 2007

Our Great Escape

It had been a lonely winter for a fourteen-year-old. I had spent the first few weeks of the vacation with my mother and stepfather in Dehra. Then they left for Delhi, and I was pretty much on my own. Of course, the servants were there to take care of my needs, but there was no one to keep me company. I would wander off in the mornings, taking some path up the hills, come back home for lunch, read a bit and then stroll off again till it was time for dinner. Sometimes I walked up to my grandparents' house, but it seemed so different now, with people I didn't know occupying the house.

The three-month winter break over, I was almost eager to return to my boarding school in Simla.

It wasn't as though I had many friends at school. I needed a friend but it was not easy to find one among a horde of rowdy, pea-shooting eighth formers, who carved their names on desks and stuck chewing gum on the class teacher's chair. Had I grown up with other children, I might have developed a taste for schoolboy anarchy; but in sharing my father's loneliness after his separation from my mother, and in being bereft of any close family ties, I had turned into a premature adult.

After a month in the eighth form I began to notice a new boy, Omar, and then only because he was a quiet, almost taciturn person who took no part in the form's feverish attempt to imitate the Marx Brothers at the circus. He showed no resentment at the prevailing anarchy: nor did he make a move to participate in it. Once he caught me looking at him, and he smiled ruefully, tolerantly. Did I sense another adult in the class? Someone who was a little older than his years?

Even before we began talking to each other, Omar and I developed an understanding of sorts, and we'd nod almost respectfully to each other when we met in the classroom corridors or the environs of the dining hall or the dormitory. We were not in the same house. The house system practised its own form of apartheid, whereby a member of one House was not expected to fraternise with someone belonging to another. Those public schools certainly knew how to clamp you into compartments. However, these barriers vanished when Omar and I found ourselves selected for the School Colts' hockey team, Omar as a full-back, I as the goalkeeper.

The taciturn Omar now spoke to me occasionally, and we combined well on the field of play. A good understanding is needed between a goalkeeper and a full-back. We were on the same wavelength. I anticipated his moves, he was familiar with mine. Years later, when I read Conrad's *The Secret Sharer*, I thought of Omar.

It wasn't until we were away from the confines of school, classroom and dining hall that our friendship flourished. The hockey team travelled to Sanawar on the next mountain range, where we were to play a couple of matches against our old rivals, the Lawrence Royal Military School. This had been my father's old school, so I was keen to explore its grounds and peep into its classrooms.

Omar and I were thrown together a good deal during the visit to Sanawar, and in our more leisurely moments, strolling undisturbed around a school where we were guests and not pupils, we exchanged life histories and other confidences. Omar, too, had lost his father—had I sensed that before?—shot in some tribal encounter on the Frontier, for he hailed from the lawless lands beyond Peshawar. A wealthy uncle was seeing to Omar's education.

We wandered into the school chapel, and there I found my father's name—A. A. Bond—on the school's roll of honour board: old boys who had lost their lives while serving during the two World Wars.

'What did his initials stand for?' asked Omar. 'Aubrey Alexander.'

'Unusual names, like yours. Why did your parents call you Rusty?'

'I am not sure.' I told him about the book I was writing. It was my first one and was called *Nine Months* (the length of the school term, not a pregnancy), and it described some of the happenings at school and lampooned a few of our teachers. I had filled three slim exercise books with this premature literary project, and I allowed Omar to go through them. He must have been my first reader and critic. They're very interesting,' he said, 'but you'll get into trouble if someone finds them, especially Mr Fisher.'

I have to admit it wasn't great literature. I was better at hockey and football. I made some spectacular saves, and we won our matches against Sanawar. When we returned to Simla, we were school heroes for a couple of days and lost some of our reticence; we were even a little more forthcoming with other boys. And then Mr Fisher, my housemaster, discovered my literary opus, *Nine Months*, under my mattress, and took it away and read it (as he told me later) from cover to cover. Corporal punishment then being in vogue, I was given six of the best with a springy Malacca cane, and my manuscript was torn up and deposited in Mr Fisher's waste-paper basket. All I had to show for my efforts were some purple welts on my bottom. These were proudly displayed to all who were interested, and I was a hero for another two days.

'Will you go away too when the British leave India?' Omar asked me one day.

I' don't think so,' I said. 'I don't have anyone to go back to in England, and my guardian, Mr Harrison, too seems to have no intention of going back.'

'Everyone is saying that our leaders and the British are going to divide the country. Simla will be in India, Peshawar in Pakistan!'

'Oh, it won't happen,' I said glibly. 'How can they cut up such a big country?' But even as we chatted about the possibility, Nehru, Jinnah and Mountbatten, and all those who mattered, were preparing their instruments for major surgery.

Before their decision impinged on our lives and everyone else's, we found a little freedom of our own, in an underground tunnel that we discovered below the third flat.

It was really part of an old, disused drainage system, and when Omar and I began exploring it, we had no idea just how far it extended. After crawling along on our bellies for some twenty feet, we found ourselves in complete darkness. Omar had brought along a small pencil torch, and with its help we continued writhing forward (moving backwards would have been quite impossible) until we saw a glimmer of light at the end of the tunnel. Dusty, musty, very scruffy, we emerged at last on to a grassy knoll, a little way outside the school boundary.

It's always a great thrill to escape beyond the boundaries that adults have devised. Here we were in unknown territory. To travel without passports—that would be the ultimate in freedom!

But more passports were on their way—and more boundaries.

Lord Mountbatten, viceroy and governor-general-to-be, came for our Founder's Day and gave away the prizes. I had won a prize for something or the other, and mounted the rostrum to receive my book from this towering, handsome man in his pinstripe suit. Bishop Cotton's was then the premier school of India, often referred to as the 'Eton of the East'. Viceroys and governors had graced its functions. Many of its boys had gone on to eminence in the civil services and armed forces. There was one 'old boy' about whom they maintained a stolid silence—General Dyer, who had ordered the massacre at Amritsar and destroyed the trust that had been building up between Britain and India.

Now Mountbatten spoke of the momentous events that were happening all around us—the War had just come to an end, the United Nations held out the promise of a world living in peace and harmony, and India, an equal partner with Britain, would be among the great nations...

A few weeks later, Bengal and the Punjab provinces were bisected. Riots flared up across northern India, and there was a great exodus of people crossing the newly-drawn frontiers of Pakistan and India. Homes were destroyed, thousands lost their lives.

The common-room radio and the occasional newspaper kept us abreast of events, but in our tunnel, Omar and I felt immune from all that was happening, worlds away from all the pillage, murder and revenge. And outside the tunnel, on the pine knoll below the school, there was fresh untrodden grass, sprinkled with clover and daisies; the only sounds we heard were the hammering of a woodpecker and the distant insistent call of the Himalayan barbet. Who could touch us there?

'And when all the wars are done,' I said, 'a butterfly will still be beautiful.'

'Did you read that somewhere?'

'No, it just came into my head.'

'Already you're a writer.'

'No, I want to play hockey for India or football for Arsenal. Only wining teams!'

'You can't win forever. Better to be a writer.'

When the monsoon arrived, the tunnel was flooded, the drain choked with rubble. We were allowed out to the cinema to see Laurence Olivier's *Hamlet*, a film that did nothing to raise our spirits on a wet and gloomy afternoon; but it was our last picture that year, because communal riots suddenly broke out in Simla's Lower Bazaar, an area that was still much as Kipling had described it—'a man who knows his way there can defy all the police of India's summer capital'—and we were confined to school indefinitely.

One morning after prayers in the chapel, the headmaster announced that the Muslim boys—those who had their homes in what was now Pakistan—would have to be evacuated, sent to their homes across the border with an armed convoy.

The tunnel no longer provided an escape for us. The bazaar was out of bounds. The flooded playing field was deserted. Omar and I sat on a damp wooden bench and talked about the future in vaguely hopeful terms; but we didn't solve any problems. Mountbatten and Nehru and Jinnah were doing all the solving.

It was soon time for Omar to leave—he left along with some fifty other boys from Lahore, Pindi and Peshawar. The rest of us—Hindus, Christians, Parsis—helped them load their luggage into the waiting trucks. A couple of boys broke down and wept. So did our departing school captain, a Pathan who had been known for his stoic and unemotional demeanour. Omar waved cheerfully to me and I waved back. We had vowed to meet again some day.

The convoy got through safely enough. There was only one casualty—the school cook, who had strayed into an off-limits area in the foothill-town of Kalika and been set upon by a mob. He wasn't seen again.

Towards the end of the school year, just as we were all getting ready to leave for the school holidays, I received a letter from Omar. He told me something about his new school and how he missed my company and our games and our tunnel to freedom. I replied and gave him my home address, but I did not hear from him again.

Some seventeen or eighteen years later I did get news of Omar, but in an entirely different context. India and Pakistan were at war, and in a bombing raid over Ambala, not far from Simla, a Pakistani plane was shot down. Its crew died in the crash. One of them, I learnt later, was Omar.

Did he, I wonder, get a glimpse of the playing fields we knew so well as boys? Perhaps memories of his schooldays flooded back as he flew over the foothills. Perhaps he remembered the tunnel through which we were able to make our little escape to freedom.

But there are no tunnels in the sky.

Gone Fishing

The house was called 'Undercliff', because that's where it stood—under a cliff. The man who went away—the owner of the house—was Robert Astley. And the man who stayed behind—the old family retainer—was Prem Bahadur.

Astley had been gone many years. He was still a bachelor in his late thirties when he'd suddenly decided that he wanted adventure, romance, faraway places; and he'd given the keys of the house to Prem Bahadur—who'd served the family for thirty years—and had set off on his travels.

Someone saw him in Sri Lanka. He'd been heard of in Burma, around the ruby mines at Mogok. Then he turned up in Java, seeking a passage through the Sunda Straits. After that the trail petered out. Years passed. The house in the hill-station remained empty.

But Prem Bahadur was still there, living in an outhouse.

Every day he opened up Undercliff, dusted the furniture in all the rooms, made sure that the bedsheets and pillowcases were clean, and set out Astley's dressing-gown and slippers.

In the old days, whenever Astley had come home after a journey or a long tramp in the hills, he had liked to bathe and change into his gown and slippers, no matter what the hour. Prem Bahadur still kept them ready. He was convinced that Robert would return one day.

Astley himself had said so.

'Keep everything ready for me, Prem, old chap. I may be back after a year, or two years, or even longer, but I'll be back, I promise you. On the first of every month I want you to go to my lawyer, Mr Kapoor. He'll give you your salary and any money that's needed for the rates and repairs. I want you to keep the house tip-top!'

'Will you bring back a wife, Sahib?'

'Lord, no! Whatever put that idea in your head?'

'I thought, perhaps—because you wanted the house kept ready....'

'Ready for me, Prem. I don't want to come home and find the old place falling down.'

And so Prem had taken care of the house—although there was no news from Astley. What had happened to him? The mystery provided a talking-point whenever local people met on the Mall. And in the bazaar the shopkeepers missed Astley because he was a man who spent freely.

His relatives still believed him to be alive. Only a few months back a brother had turned up—a brother who had a farm in Canada and could not stay in India for long. He had deposited a further sum with the lawyer and told Prem to carry on as before. The salary provided Prem with his few needs. Moreover, he was convinced that Robert would return.

Another man might have neglected the house and grounds, but not Prem Bahadur. He had a genuine regard for the absent owner. Prem was much older—now almost sixty and none too strong, suffering from pleurisy and other chest troubles—but he remembered Robert as both a boy and a young man. They had been together on numerous hunting and fishing trips in the mountains. They had slept out under the stars, bathed in icy mountain streams, and eaten from the same cooking-pot. Once, when crossing a small river, they had been swept downstream by a flash-flood, a wall of water that came thundering down the gorges without any warning during the rainy season. Together they had struggled back to safety. Back in the hill-station, Astley told everyone that Prem had saved his life; while Prem was equally insistent that he owed his life to Robert.

This year the monsoon had begun early and ended late. It dragged on through most of September, and Prem Bahadur's cough grew worse and his breathing more difficult.

He lay on his charpai on the veranda, staring out at the garden, which was beginning to get out of hand, a tangle of dahlias, snake-lilies and convolvulus. The sun finally came out. The wind shifted from the south-west to the north-west, and swept the clouds away.

Prem Bahadur had taken his charpai into the garden, and was lying in the sun, puffing at his small hookah, when he saw Robert Astley at the gate.

He tried to get up but his legs would not oblige him. The hookah slipped from his hand.

Astley came walking down the garden path and stopped in front of the old retainer, smiling down at him. He did not look a day older than when Prem Bahadur had last seen him.

'So you have come at last,' said Prem.

'I told you I'd return.'

'It has been many years. But you have not changed.'

'Nor have you, old chap.'

'I have grown old and sick and feeble.'

'You'll be fine now. That's why I've come.'

'I'll open the house,' said Prem, and this time he found himself getting up quite easily.

'It isn't necessary,' said Astley.

'But all is ready for you!'

'I know. I have heard of how well you have looked after everything. Come then, let's take a last look round. We cannot stay, you know.'

Prem was a little mystified but he opened the front door and took Robert through the drawing-room and up the stairs to the bedroom. Robert saw the dressing-gown and the slippers, and he placed his hand gently on the old man's shoulder.

When they returned downstairs and emerged into the sunlight, Prem was surprised to see himself—or rather his skinny body—stretched out on the charpai. The hookah lay on the ground, where it had fallen.

Prem looked at Astley in bewilderment.

'But who is that—lying there?'

'It was you. Only the husk now, the empty shell. This is the real you, standing here beside me.'

'You came for me?'

'I couldn't come until you were ready. As for me, I left *my* shell a long time ago. But you were determined to hang on, keeping this house together. Are you ready now?'

'And the house?'

'Others will live in it. Nothing is lost for ever, everything begins again. ... But come, it's time to go fishing....'

Astley took Prem by the arm, and they walked through the dappled sunlight under the deodars and finally left that place for another.

Susanna's Seven Husbands

Locally, the tomb was known as 'the grave of the seven-times married one'.

You'd be forgiven for thinking it was Bluebeard's grave; he was reputed to have killed several wives in turn because they showed undue curiosity about a locked room. But this was the tomb of Susanna Anna-Maria Yeates, and the inscription (most of it in Latin) stated that she was mourned by all who had benefited from her generosity, her beneficiaries having included various schools, orphanages, and the church across the road. There was no sign of any other graves in the vicinity, and presumably her husbands had been interred in the old Rajpur graveyard, below the Delhi Ridge.

I was still in my teens when I first saw the ruins of what had once been a spacious and handsome mansion. Desolate and silent, its well-laid paths were overgrown with weeds, its flower-beds had disappeared under a growth of thorny jungle. The two-storeyed house had looked across the Grand Trunk Road. Now abandoned, feared and shunned, it stood encircled in mystery, reputedly the home of evil spirits.

Outside the gate, along the Grand Trunk Road, thousands of vehicles sped by—cars, trucks, buses, tractors, bullock-carts—but few noticed the old mansion or its mausoleum, set back as they were from the main road, hidden by mango, neem and peepul trees. One old and massive peepul tree grew out of the ruins of the house, strangling it much as its owner was said to have strangled one of her dispensable paramours.

As a much married person with a quaint habit of disposing of her husbands, whenever she tired of them, Susanna's malignant spirit was said to haunt the deserted garden. I had examined the tomb, I had gazed upon the ruins, I had scrambled through shrubbery and overgrown rose-bushes, but I had not encountered the spirit of this mysterious woman. Perhaps, at the time, I was too pure and innocent to be targeted by malignant spirits. For, malignant she must have been, if the stories about her were true.

No one had been down into the vaults of the ruined mansion. They were said to be occupied by a family of cobras, traditional guardians of buried treasure. Had she really been a woman of great wealth, and could treasure still be buried there? I put these questions to Naushad, the furniture-maker, who had lived in the vicinity all his life, and whose father had made the furniture and fittings for this and other great houses in Old Delhi.

'Lady Susanna, as she was known, was much sought after for her wealth,'recalled Naushad. She was no miser, either. She spent freely, reigning in state in her palatial home, with many horses and carriages at her disposal. You see the stables there, behind the ruins? Now, they are occupied by bats and jackals. Every evening she rode through the Roshanara Gardens, the cynosure of all eyes, for she was beautiful as well as wealthy. Yes, all men sought her favours, and she could choose from the best of them. Many were fortune-hunters. She did not discourage them. Some found favour for a time, but she soon tired of them. None of her husbands enjoyed her wealth for very long!

'Today, no one enters those ruins, where once there was mirth and laughter. She was the zamindari lady, the owner of much land, and she administered her estate with a strong hand. She was kind if rents were paid when they fell due, but terrible if someone failed to pay.'

'Well, over fifty years have gone by since she was laid to rest, but still men speak of her with awe. Her spirit is restless, and it is said that she often visits the scenes of her former splendour. She has been seen walking through this gate, or riding in the gardens, or driving in her phaeton down the Rajpur road.'

'And, what happened to all those husbands?' I asked.

'Most of them died mysterious deaths. Even the doctors were baffled. Tomkins Sahib drank too much. The lady soon tired of him. A drunken husband is a burdensome creature, she was heard to say. He would have drunk himself to death, but she was an impatient woman and was anxious to replace him. You see those datura bushes growing wild in the grounds? They have always done well here.'

'Belladonna?' I suggested.

'That's right, huzoor. Introduced in the whisky-soda, they put him to sleep for ever.'

'She was quite humane in her way.'

'Oh, very humane, sir. She hated to see anyone suffer. One sahib, I don't know his name, drowned in the tank behind the house, where the water-lilies grew. But she made sure he was half-dead before he fell in. She had large, powerful hands, they said.'

'Why did she bother to marry them? Couldn't she just have had men friends?'

'Not in those days, dear sir. Respectable society would not have tolerated it. Neither in India nor in the West would it have been permitted.'

'She was born out of her time,' I remarked.

'True, sir. And remember, most of them were fortune-hunters. So, we need not waste too much pity on them.'

'*She* did not waste any.'

'She was without pity. Especially when she found out what they were really after. The snakes had a better chance of survival.'

'How did the other husbands take their leave of this world?'

'Well, the Colonel-sahib shot himself while cleaning his rifle. Purely an accident, huzoor. Although some say she had loaded his gun without his knowledge. Such was her reputation by now that she was suspected even when innocent. But she bought her way out of trouble. It was easy enough, if you were wealthy.'

'And, the fourth husband?'

'Oh, he died a natural death. There was a cholera epidemic that year, and he was carried off by the haija. Although, again, there were some who said that a good dose of arsenic produced the same symptoms! Anyway, it was cholera on the death certificate. And, the doctor who signed it was the next to marry her.'

'Being a doctor, he was probably quite careful about what he ate and drank.

'He lasted about a year.'

'What happened?'

'He was bitten by a cobra.'

'Well, that was just bad luck, wasn't it? You could hardly blame it on Susanna.'

'No, huzoor, but the cobra was in his bedroom. It was coiled around the bed-post. And, when he undressed for the night, it struck! He was dead when Susanna came into the room an hour later. She had a way with snakes. She did not harm them and they never attacked her.'

'And, there were no antidotes in those days. Exit the doctor. Who was the sixth husband?'

'A handsome man. An indigo planter. He had gone bankrupt when the indigo trade came to an end. He was hoping to recover his fortune with the good lady's help. But our Susanna-mem, she did not believe in sharing her fortune with anyone.'

'How did she remove the indigo planter?'

'It was said that she lavished strong drink upon him, and when he lay helpless, she assisted him on the road we all have to take by pouring molten lead in his ears.'

'A painless death, I'm told.'

'But a terrible price to pay huzoor, simply because one is no longer needed....'

We walked along the dusty highway, enjoying the evening breeze, and some time later we entered the Roshanara Gardens, in those days Delhi's most popular and fashionable meeting place.

'You have told me how six of her husbands died, Naushad. I thought there were seven?'

'Ah, a gallant young magistrate, who perished right here, huzoor. They were driving through the park after dark when the lady's carriage was attacked by brigands. In defending her, the gallant young man received a fatal sword wound.'

'Not the lady's fault, Naushad.'

'No, my friend. But he was a magistrate, remember, and the assailants, one of whose relatives had been convicted by him, were out for revenge. Oddly enough, though, two of the men were given employment by the lady Susanna at a later date. You may draw your own conclusions.'

'And, were there others?'

'Not husbands. But an adventurer, a soldier of fortune came along. He found her treasure, they say. He lies buried with it, in the cellars of the ruined house. His bones lie scattered there, among gold and silver and precious jewels. The cobras guard them still! But how he perished was a mystery, and remains so till this day.'

'What happened to Susanna?'

'She lived to a good old age, as you know. If she paid for her crimes, it wasn't in this life! As you know, she had no children. But she started an orphanage and gave generously to the poor and to various schools and institutions, including a home for widows. She died peacefully in her sleep.'

'A merry widow,' I remarked. 'The Black Widow spider!'

Don't go looking for Susanna's tomb. It vanished some years ago, along with the ruins of her mansion. A smart new housing estate came up on the site, but not after several workmen and a contractor succumbed to snake bite! Occasionally, residents complain of a malignant ghost in their midst, who is given to flagging down cars, especially those driven by single men. There have been one or two mysterious disappearances. Ask anyone living along this stretch of the Delhi Ridge, and they'll tell you that's it's true.

And, after dusk, an old-fashioned horse and carriage can sometimes be seen driving through the Roshanara Gardens. Ignore it, my friend. Don't stop to answer any questions from the beautiful fair lady who smiles at you from behind lace curtains. She's still looking for a suitable husband.

On Fairy Hill

Those little green lights that I used to see, twinkling away on Pari Tibba—there had to be a scientific explanation for them, I was sure. After dark we see or hear many things that seem mysterious, irrational. And then by the clear light of day we find that the magic, the mystery has an explanation after all.

But I did see those lights occasionally—late at night, when I walked home from town to my little cottage at the edge of the forest. They moved too fast for them to be torches or lanterns carried by people. And as there were no roads on Pari Tibba, they could not have been cycle or cart lamps. Someone told me there was phosphorus in the rocks, and that this probably accounted for the luminous glow emanating from the hillside late at night. Possibly; but I was not convinced.

My encounter with the little people happened by the light of day.

One morning, early in April, purely on an impulse I decided to climb to the top of Pari Tibba and look around for myself. It was springtime in the Himalayan foothills. The sap was rising—in the trees, in the grass, in the wildflowers, in my own veins. I took the path through the oak forest, down to the little steam at the bottom of the hill, and then up the steep slope of Pari Tibba, hill of the fairies.

It was quite a scramble getting to the top. The path ended at the stream. After that, I had to clutch at brambles and tufts of grass to make the ascent. Fallen pine needles, slippery underfoot, made it difficult to get a foothold. But finally I made it to the top—a grassy plateau fringed by pines and a few wild medlar trees now clothed in white blossom.

It was a pretty spot. And as I was hot and sweaty, I removed most of my clothing and lay down under a medlar to rest. The climb had been quite tiring. But a fresh breeze soon brought me back to life. It made a soft humming sound in the pines. And the grass, sprinkled with yellow buttercups, buzzed with the sound of crickets and grasshoppers.

After some time I stood up and surveyed the scene. To the north, Landour with its rusty red-roofed cottages; to the south, the wide valley and a silver stream flowing towards the Ganga. To the west, rolling hills, patches of forest, and a small village tucked into a fold of the mountain.

Disturbed by my presence, a barking-deer ran across the clearing and down the opposite slope. A band of long-tailed blue magpies rose from the oak trees, glided across the knoll, and settled in another strand of oaks.

I was alone. Alone with the wind and the sky. It had probably been months, possibly years, since any human had passed that way. The soft lush grass looked most inviting. I lay down again on the sun-warmed sward. Pressed and bruised by my weight, catmint and clover gave out a soft fragrance. A ladybird climbed up my leg and began to explore my body. A swarm of white butterflies fluttered around me.

I slept.

I have no idea how long I slept, but when I awoke it was to experience an unusual, soothing sensation all over my limbs, as though they were being gently stroked with rose-petals.

All lethargy gone, I opened my eyes to find a little girl—or was it a woman? —about two inches high, sitting cross-legged on my chest and studying me intently. Her hair fell in long black tresses. Her skin was the colour of honey. Her firm little breasts were like tiny acorns. She held a buttercup, larger than her hand, and with it she was stroking my tingling flesh.

I was tingling all over. A sensation of sensual joy surged through my limbs.

A tiny boy—man?—completely naked, now joined the elfin girl, and they held hands and looked into my eyes, smiling, their teeth little pearls, their lips soft petals of apricot blossom. Were these the nature spirits, the flower fairies, I had often dreamt of? I raised my head and saw that there were scores of little people all over me—exploring my legs, thighs, waist and arms. Delicate, caring, gentle, caressing creatures. They wanted to love me!

Some of them were laving me with dew or pollen or some soft essence. I closed my eyes. Waves of pure physical pleasure swept over me. I had never known anything like it. My limbs turned to water. The sky revolved around me, and I must have fainted.

When I awoke, perhaps an hour later, the little people had gone. A fragrance of honeysuckle lingered in the air. A deep rumble overhead made me look up. Dark clouds had gathered, threatening rain. Had the thunder frightened them away, to their abode beneath the rocks and tree-roots? Or had they simply tired of sporting with a strange newcomer? Mischievous they were; for when I looked around for my clothes I could not find them anywhere.

A wave of panic surged over me. I ran here and there, looking behind shrubs and tree-trunks, but to no avail. My clothes had disappeared, along with the fairies—if, indeed, they were fairies!

It began to rain. Large drops cannoned off the dry rocks. Then it hailed and soon the slope was covered with ice. There was no shelter. Naked, I ran down the path to the stream. There was no one to see me—only a wild mountain-goat, speeding away in the opposite direction. Gusts of wind slashed rain and hail across my face and body. Panting and shivering, I took shelter beneath an overhanging rock until the storm had passed. By then it was almost dusk and I was able to ascend the path to my cottage without encountering anyone, apart from a band of startled langoors, who chattered excitedly on seeing me.

I couldn't stop shivering, so I went straight to bed. I slept a deep, dreamless sleep and woke up the next morning with a high fever.

Mechanically I dressed, made myself some breakfast and tried to get through the morning's chores. When I took my temperature I found it was a hundred and four. So I swallowed a tablet and went back to bed.

There I lay until late afternoon, when the postman's knocking woke me. I left my letters unopened on my desk (that in itself was unusual) and returned to my bed.

The fever lasted almost a week and left me weak and half-starved. I couldn't have climbed Pari Tibba again, even if I'd wanted to; but I reclined on my window-seat and looked at the clouds drifting over that desolate hill. Desolate it seemed, and yet strangely inhabited. When it grew dark, I waited for those little green fairy lights to appear; but these, it seemed, were now to be denied to me.

And so I returned to my desk, my typewriter, my newspaper articles and correspondence. It was a lonely period in my life. My marriage hadn't worked out: my wife, fond of high society and averse to living with an unsuccessful writer in a remote cottage in the woods, was following her own, more successful career in Mumbai. I had always been rather half-hearted in my approach to making money, whereas she had always wanted more and more of it. She left me—left me with my books and my dreams....

Had it all been a dream, that strange episode on Pari Tibba? Had an over-active imagination conjured up those aerial spirits, those Siddhas of the Upper Air? Or were they underground people, living deep within the bowels of the hill? If I was going to keep my sanity I knew I had better get on with the more mundane aspects of living—such as going into town to buy my groceries, mending the leaking roof, paying the electricity bill, plodding up to the post office, and remembering to deposit the odd cheque that came my way. All the mundane things that made life so dull and dreary.

The truth is, what we commonly call life is not life at all. Its routine and settled ways are the curse of life, and we will do almost anything to get away from the trivial, even if it is only for a few hours of forgetfulness in alcohol, drugs, forbidden sex, or golf. Some of us would even go underground with the fairies, those little people who have sought refuge in Mother Earth from mankind's killing ways; for they are as vulnerable as butterflies and flowers. All things beautiful are easily destroyed.

I am sitting at my window in the gathering dark, penning these stray thoughts, when I see them coming—hand in hand, walking on a swirl of mist, radiant, suffused with all the colours of the rainbow. For a rainbow has formed a bridge from them, from Pari Tibba, to the edge of my window.

I am ready to go, to love and be loved, in their secret lairs or in the upper air—far from the stifling confines of the world in which we toil....

Come, fairies, carry me away, to love me as you did that summer's day!

•

The Overcoat

It was clear frosty weather, and as the moon came up over the Himalayan peaks, I could see that patches of snow still lay on the roads of the hill-station. I would have been quite happy in bed, with a book and a hot-water bottle at my side, but I'd promised the Kapadias that I'd go to their party, and I felt it would be churlish of me to stay away. I put on two sweaters, an old football scarf, and an overcoat, and set off down the moonlit road.

It was a walk of just over a mile to the Kapadias' house, and I had covered about half the distance when I saw a girl standing in the middle of the road.

She must have been sixteen or seventeen. She looked rather old-fashioned—long hair, hanging to her waist, and a flummoxy sequined dress, pink and lavender, that reminded me of the photos in my Grandmother's family album. When I went closer, I noticed that she had lovely eyes and a winning smile.

'Good evening,' I said. 'It's a cold night to be out.' 'Are you going to the party?' she asked.

'That's right. And I can see from your lovely dress that you're going, too. Come along, we're nearly there.'

She fell into step beside me and we soon saw lights from the Kapadias' house shining brightly through the deodars. The girl told me her name was Julie. I hadn't seen her before but, then, I'd only been in the hill-station a few months.

There was quite a crowd at the party, and no one seemed to know Julie. Everyone thought she was a friend of mine. I did not deny it. Obviously she was someone who was feeling lonely and wanted to be friendly with people. And she was certainly enjoying herself. I did not see her do much eating or drinking, but she flitted about from one group to another, talking, listening, laughing; and when the music began, she was dancing almost continuously, alone or with partners, it didn't matter which, she was completely wrapped up in the music.

It was almost midnight when I got up to go. I had drunk a fair amount of punch, and I was ready for bed. As I was saying goodnight to my hosts and wishing everyone a merry Christmas, Julie slipped her arm into mine and said she'd be going home, too.

When we were outside I said, 'Where do you live, Julie?'

'At Wolfsburn,' she said. 'At the top of the hill.'

'There's a cold wind,' I said. 'And although your dress is beautiful, it doesn't look very warm. Here, you'd better wear my overcoat. I've plenty of protection.'

She did not protest, and allowed me to slip my overcoat over her shoulders. Then we started out on the walk home. But I did not have to escort her all the way. At about the spot where we had met, she said, 'There's a short cut from here. I'll just scramble up the hillside.'

'Do you know it well?' I asked. 'It's a very narrow path.'

'Oh, I know every stone on the path. I use it all the time. And besides, it's a really bright night.'

'Well, keep the coat on,' I said. 'I can collect it tomorrow.'

She hesitated for a moment, then smiled and nodded to me. She then disappeared up the hill, and I went home alone.

The next day I walked up to Wolfsburn. I crossed a little brook, from which the house had probably got its name, and entered an open iron gate. But of the house itself little remained. Just a roofless ruin, a pile of stones, a shattered chimney, a few Doric pillars where a verandah had once stood.

Had Julie played a joke on me? Or had I found the wrong house?

I walked around the hill to the mission house where the Taylors lived, and asked old Mrs Taylor if she knew a girl called Julie.

'No, I don't think so,' she said. 'Where does she live?' 'At Wolfsburn, I was told. But the house is just a ruin.'

'Nobody has lived at Wolfsburn for over forty years. The Mackinnons lived there. One of the old families who settled here. But when their girl died....' She stopped and gave me a queer look. 'I think her name was Julie...Anyway, when she died, they sold the house and went away. No one ever lived in it again, and it fell into decay. But it couldn't be the same Julie you're looking for. She died of consumption—there wasn't much you could do about it in those days. Her grave is in the cemetery, just down the road.'

I thanked Mrs Taylor and walked slowly down the road to the cemetery: not really wanting to know any more, but propelled forward almost against my will.

It was a small cemetery under the deodars. You could see the eternal snows of the Himalayas standing out against the pristine blue of the sky. Here lay the bones of forgotten Empire-builders—soldiers, merchants, adventurers, their wives and children. It did not take me long to find Julie's grave. It had a simple headstone with her name clearly outlined on it:

Julie Mackinnon
1923-39
'With us one moment,
Taken the next
Gone to her Maker,
Gone to her rest.

Although many monsoons had swept across the cemetery wearing down the stones, they had not touched this little tombstone.

I was turning to leave when I caught a glimpse of something familiar behind the headstone. I walked round to where it lay.

Neatly folded on the grass was my overcoat.

Do You Believe in Ghosts?

'Do you believe in ghosts?'
Asked the passenger
On platform number three.
'I'm a rational man,' said I,
'I believe in what I can see—
Your hands, your feet, your beard!'
'Then look again,' said he,
And promptly disappeared!

A Face in the Dark

It may give you some idea of rural humour if I begin this tale with an anecdote that concerns me. I was walking alone through a village at night when I met an old man carrying a lantern. I found, to my surprise, that the man was blind. 'Old man' I asked, 'if you cannot see, why do you carry a lamp?'

'I carry this,' he replied, 'so that fools do not stumble against me in the dark.'

This incident has only a slight connection with the story that follows, but I think it provides the right sort of tone and setting. Mr Oliver, an Anglo-Indian teacher, was returning to his school late one night, on the outskirts of the hill-station of Simla. The school was conducted on English public school lines and the boys, most of them from well-to-do Indian families, wore blazers, caps, and ties. *Life* magazine, in a feature on India had once called this school the 'Eton of the East'.

Individuality was not encouraged; they were all destined to become 'leaders of men'.

Mr Oliver had been teaching in the school for several years. Sometimes it seemed like an eternity; for one day followed another with the same monotonous routine. The Simla bazaar, with its cinemas and restaurants, was about two miles from the school; and Mr Oliver, a bachelor, usually strolled into the town in the evening, returning after dark, when he would take a short cut through a pine forest.

When there was a strong wind, the pine trees made sad, eerie sounds that kept most people to the main road. But Mr Oliver was not a nervous or imaginative man. He carried a torch and, on the night I write of, its pale gleam—the batteries were running down—moved fitfully over the narrow forest path. When its flickering light fell on the figure of a boy, who was sitting alone on a rock, Mr Oliver stopped. Boys were not supposed to be out of school after 7 p.m., and it was now well past nine.

'What are you doing out here, boy?' asked Mr Oliver sharply, moving closer so that he could recognise the miscreant. But even as he approached the boy, Mr Oliver sensed that something was wrong. The boy appeared to be crying. His head hung down, he held his face in his hands, and his body shook convulsively. It was a strange, soundless weeping, and Mr Oliver felt distinctly uneasy

'Well—what's the matter?' he asked, his anger giving way to concern. 'What are you crying for?' The boy would not answer or look up. His body continued to be racked with silent sobbing.

'Come on, boy, you shouldn't be out here at this hour. Tell me the trouble. Look up!'

The boy looked up. He took his hands from his face and looked up at his teacher. The light from Mr Oliver's torch fell on the boy's face—if you could call it a face.

He had no eyes, ears, nose, or mouth. It was just a round smooth head—with a school cap on top of it. And that's where the story should end—as indeed it has for several people who have had similar experiences and dropped dead of inexplicable heart attacks. But for Mr Oliver it did not end there.

The torch fell from his trembling hand. He turned and scrambled down the path, running blindly through the trees and calling for help. He was still running towards the school buildings when he saw a lantern swinging in the middle of the path. Mr Oliver had never before been so pleased to see the night-watchman. He stumbled up to the watchman, gasping for breath and speaking incoherently.

'What is it, Sir?' asked the watchman. 'Has there been an accident? Why are you running?'

'I saw something—something horrible—a boy weeping in the forest—and he had no face!'

'No face, Sir?'

'No eyes, nose, mouth—nothing.'

'Do you mean it was like this, Sir?' asked the watchman, and raised the lamp to his own face. The watchman had no eyes, no ears, no features at all—not even an eyebrow!

The wind blew the lamp out, and Mr Oliver had his heart attack.

The Eyes of the Eagle

It was a high, piercing sound, almost like the yelping of a dog. Jai stopped picking the wild strawberries that grew in the grass around him, and looked up at the sky. He had a dog—a shaggy guard-dog called Motu—but Motu did not yet yelp, he growled and barked. The strange sound came from the sky, and Jai had heard it before. Now, realising what it was, he jumped to his feet, calling to his dog, calling his sheep to start for home. Motu came bounding towards him, ready for a game.

'Not now, Motu!' said Jai. 'We must get the lambs home quickly.' Again he looked up at the sky.

He saw it now, a black speck against the sun, growing larger as it circled the mountain, coming lower every moment—a Golden Eagle, king of the skies over the higher Himalayas, ready now to swoop and seize its prey.

Had it seen a pheasant or a pine marten? Or was it after one of the lambs? Jai had never lost a lamb to an eagle, but recently some of the other shepherds had been talking about a golden eagle that had been preying on their flocks.

The sheep had wandered some way down the side of the mountain, and Jai ran after them to make sure that none of the lambs had gone off on its own.

Motu ran about, barking furiously. He wasn't very good at keeping the sheep together—he was often bumping into them and sending them tumbling down the slope—but his size and bear-like look kept the leopards and wolves at a distance.

Jai was counting the lambs; they were bleating loudly and staying close to their mothers. *One—two—three—four*...

There should have been a fifth. Jai couldn't see it on the slope below him. He looked up towards a rocky ledge near the steep path to the Tung temple. The golden eagle was circling the rocks.

The bird disappeared from sight for a moment, then rose again with a small creature grasped firmly in its terrible talons.

'It has taken a lamb!' shouted Jai. He started scrambling up the slope. Motu ran ahead of him, barking furiously at the big bird as it glided away over the tops of the stunted junipers to its eyrie on the cliffs above Tung.

There was nothing that Jai and Motu could do except stare helplessly and angrily at the disappearing eagle. The lamb had died the instant it had been struck. The rest of the flock seemed unaware of what had happened. They still grazed on the thick, sweet grass of the mountain slopes.

'We had better drive them home, Motu,' said Jai, and at a nod from the boy, the big dog bounded down the slope, to take part in his favourite game of driving the sheep homewards. Soon he had them running all over the place, and Jai had to dash about trying to keep them together. Finally they straggled homewards.

'A fine lamb gone,' said Jai to himself gloomily. 'I wonder what Grandfather will say.'

Grandfather said, 'Never mind. It had to happen some day. That eagle has been watching the sheep for some time.'

Grandmother, more practical, said; 'We could have sold the lamb for three hundred rupees. You'll have to be more careful in future, Jai. Don't fall asleep on the hillside, and don't read story-books when you are supposed to be watching the sheep!'

'I wasn't reading this morning,' said Jai truthfully, forgetting to mention that he had been gathering strawberries.

'It's good for him to read,' said Grandfather, who had never had the luck to go to school. In his days, there weren't any schools in the mountains. Now there was one in every village.

'Time enough to read at night,' said Grandmother, who did not think much of the little one-room school down at Maku, their home village.

'Well, these are the October holidays,' said Grandfather. 'Otherwise he would not be here to help us with the sheep. It will snow by the end of the month, and then we will move with the flock. You will have more time for reading then, Jai.'

At Maku, which was down in the warmer valley, Jai's parents tilled a few narrow terraces on which they grew barley, millets and potatoes. The old people brought their sheep up to the Tung meadows to graze during the summer months. They stayed in a small stone hut just off the path which pilgrims took to the ancient temple. At 12,000 feet above sea level, it was the highest Hindu temple on the inner Himalayan ranges.

The following day Jai and Motu were very careful. The did not let the sheep out of sight even for a minute. Nor did they catch sight of the golden eagle. 'What if it attacks again?' wondered Jai. 'How will I stop it?'

The great eagle, with its powerful beak and talons, was more than a match for boy or dog. Its hind claw, four inches round the curve, was its most dangerous weapon. When it spread its wings, the distance from tip to tip was more than eight feet.

The eagle did not come that day because it had fed well and was now resting in its eyrie. Old bones, which had belonged to pheasants, snow-cocks, pine martens and even foxes, were scattered about the rocks which formed the eagle's home. The eagle had a mate, but it was not the breeding season and she was away on a scouting expedition of her own.

The golden eagle stood on its rocky ledge, staring majestically across the valley. Its hard, unblinking eyes missed nothing. Those strange orange-yellow eyes could spot a field-rat or a mouse-hare more than a hundred yards below.

There were other eagles on the mountain, but usually they kept to their own territory. And only the bolder ones went for lambs, because the flocks were always protected by men and dogs.

The eagle took off from its eyrie and glided gracefully, powerfully over the valley, circling the Tung mountain.

Below lay the old temple, built from slabs of grey granite. A line of pilgrims snaked up the steep, narrow path. On the meadows below the peak, the sheep grazed peacefully, unaware of the presence of the eagle. The great bird's shadow slid over the sunlit slopes.

The eagle saw the boy and the dog, but he did not fear them. He had his eye on a lamb that was frisking about on the grass, a few feet away from the other grazing sheep.

Jai did not see the eagle until it swept round an outcrop of rocks about a hundred feet away. It moved silently, without any movement of its wings, for it had already built up the momentum for its dive. Now it came straight at the lamb.

Motu saw the bird in time. With a low growl he dashed forward and reached the side of the lamb at almost the same instant that the eagle swept in.

There was a terrific collision. Feathers flew. The eagle screamed with rage. The lamb tumbled down the slope, and Motu howled in pain as the huge beak struck him high on the leg.

The big bird, a little stunned by the clash, flew off rather unsteadily, with a mighty beating of its wings.

Motu had saved the lamb. It was frightened but unhurt. Bleating loudly, it joined the other sheep, who took up the bleating. Jai ran up to Motu, who lay whimpering on the ground. There was no sign of the eagle. Quickly he removed his shirt and vest; then he wrapped his vest round the dog's wound, tying it in position with his belt.

Motu could not get up, and he was much too heavy for Jai to carry. Jai did not want to leave his dog alone, in case the eagle returned to attack.

He stood up, cupped his hand to his mouth, and began calling for his grandfather.

'Dada, dada!' he shouted, and presently Grandfather heard him and came stumbling down the slope. He was followed by another shepherd, and together they lifted Motu and carried him home.

Motu had a bad wound, but Grandmother cleaned it and applied a paste made of herbs. Then she laid strips of carrot over the wound—an old mountain remedy—and bandaged the leg. But it would be some time before Motu could run about again. By then it would probably be snowing and time to leave these high-altitude pastures and return to the valley. Meanwhile, the sheep had to be taken out to graze, and Grandfather decided to accompany Jai for the remaining period.

They did not see the golden eagle for two or three days, and, when they did, it was flying over the next range. Perhaps it had found some other source of food, or even another flock of sheep. 'Are you afraid of the eagle?' Grandfather asked Jai.

'I wasn't before,' said Jai. 'Not until it hurt Motu. I did not know it could be so dangerous. But Motu hurt it too. He banged straight into it!'

'Perhaps it won't bother us again,' said Grandfather thoughtfully. 'A bird's wing is easily injured—even an eagle's.'

Jai wasn't so sure. He had seen it strike twice, and he knew that it was not afraid of anyone. Only when it learnt to fear his presence would it keep away from the flock.

The next day Grandfather did not feel well; he was feverish and kept to his bed. Motu was hobbling about gamely on three legs; the wounded leg was still very sore.

'Don't go too far with the sheep,' said Grandmother. 'Let them graze near the house.'

'But there's hardly any grass here,' said Jai.

'I don't want you wandering off while that eagle is still around.'

'Give him my stick,' said Grandfather from his bed. Grandmother took it from the corner and handed it to the boy.

It was an old stick, made of wild cherry wood, which Grandfather often carried around. The wood was strong and well-seasoned; the stick was stout and long. It reached up to Jai's shoulders.

'Don't lose it,' said Grandfather. 'It was given to me many years ago by a wandering scholar who came to the Tung temple. I was going to give it to you when you got bigger, but perhaps this is the right time for you to have it. If the eagle comes near you, swing the stick around your head. That should frighten it off!'

Clouds had gathered over the mountains, and a heavy mist hid the Tung temple. With the approach of winter, the flow of pilgrims had been reduced to a trickle. The shepherds had started leaving the lush meadows and returning to their villages at lower altitudes. Very soon the bears and the leopards and the golden eagles would have the high ranges all to themselves.

Jai used the cherry wood stick to prod the sheep along the path until they reached the steep meadows. The stick would have to be a substitute for Motu. And they seemed to respond to it more readily than they did to Motu's mad charges.

Because of the sudden cold and the prospect of snow, Grandmother had made Jai wear a rough woollen jacket and a pair of high boots bought from a Tibetan trader. He wasn't used to the boots—he wore sandals at other times—and had some difficulty in climbing quickly up and down the hillside. It was tiring work, trying to keep the flock together. The cawing of some crows warned Jai that the eagle might be around, but the mist prevented him from seeing very far.

After some time the mist lifted and Jai was able to see the temple and the snow-peaks towering behind it. He saw the golden eagle, too. It was circling high overhead. Jai kept close to the flock—one eye on the eagle, one eye on the restless sheep.

Then the great bird stooped and flew lower. It circled the temple and then pretended to go away. Jai felt sure it would be back. And a few minutes later it reappeared from the other side of the mountain. It was much lower now, wings spread out and back, taloned feet to the fore, piercing eyes fixed on its target—a small lamb that had suddenly gone frisking down the slope, away from Jai and the flock.

Now it flew lower still, only a few feet off the ground, paying no attention to the boy.

It passed Jai with a great rush of air, and as it did so the boy struck out with his stick and caught the bird a glancing blow.

The eagle missed its prey, and the tiny lamb skipped away.

To Jai's amazement, the bird did not fly off. Instead it landed on the hillside and glared at the boy, as a king would glare at a humble subject who had dared to pelt him with a pebble.

The golden eagle stood almost as tall as Jai. Its wings were still outspread. Its fierce eyes seemed to be looking through and through the boy.

Jai's first instinct was to turn and run. But the cherry wood stick was still in his hands, and he felt sure there was power in it. He saw that the eagle was about to launch itself again at the lamb. Instead of running away, he ran forward, the stick raised above his head.

The eagle rose a few feet off the ground and struck out with its huge claws.

Luckily for Jai, his heavy jacket took the force of the blow. A talon ripped through the sleeve, and the sleeve fell away. At the same time the heavy stick caught the eagle across its open wing. The bird gave a shrill cry of pain and fury. Then it turned and flapped heavily away, flying unsteadily because of its injured wing.

Jai still clutched the stick, because he expected the bird to return; he did not even glance at his torn jacket. But the golden eagle had alighted on a distant rock and was in no hurry to return to the attack.

Jai began driving the sheep home. The clouds had become heavy and black, and presently the first snow-flakes began to fall.

Jai saw a hare go lolloping done the hill. When it was about fifty yards away, there was a rush of air from the eagle's beating wings, and Jai saw the bird approaching the hare in a sidelong drive.

'So it hasn't been badly hurt,' thought Jai, feeling a little relieved, for he could not help admiring the great bird. 'Now it has found something else to chase for its dinner.'

The hare saw the eagle and dodged about, making for a clump of junipers. Jai did not know if it was caught or not, because the snow and sleet had increased and both bird and hare were lost in the gathering snow-storm.

The sheep were bleating behind him. One of the lambs looked tired, and he stooped to pick it up. As he did so, he heard a thin, whining sound. It grew louder by the second. Before he could look up, a huge wing caught him across the shoulders and sent him sprawling. The lamb tumbled down the slope with him, into a thorny bilberry bush.

The bush saved them. Jai saw the eagle coming in again, flying low. It was another eagle! One had been vanquished, and now here was another, just as big and fearless, probably the mate of the first eagle.

Jai had lost his stick and there was no way by which he could fight the second eagle. So he crept further into the bush, holding the lamb beneath him. At the same time he began shouting at the top of his voice—both to scare the bird away and to summon help. The eagle could not easily get at them now; but the rest of the flock was exposed on the hillside. Surely the eagle would make for them.

Even as the bird circled and came back in another dive, Jai heard fierce barking. The eagle immediately swung away and rose skywards.

The barking came from Motu. Hearing Jai's shouts and sensing that something was wrong, he had come limping out of the house, ready to do battle. Behind him came another shepherd and—most wonderful of all—Grandmother herself, banging two frying-pans together. The barking, the banging and the shouting frightened the eagles away. The sheep scattered too, and it was some time before they could all be rounded up. By then it was snowing heavily.

'Tomorrow we must all go down to Maku,' said the shepherd.

'Yes, it's time we went,' said Grandmother. 'You can read your story-books again, Jai.'

'I'll have my own story to tell,' said Jai.

When they reached the hut and Jai saw Grandfather, he said, 'Oh, I've forgotten your stick!'

But Motu had picked it up. Carrying it between his teeth, he brought it home and sat down with it in the open doorway. He had decided the cherry wood was good for his teeth and would have chewed it up if Grandmother hadn't taken it from him.

'Never mind,' said Grandfather, sitting up on his cot. 'It isn't the stick that matters. It's the person who holds it.'

Bitter Gooseberries

(A tale from Burma)

This is the story of the snake and the gooseberries and much else besides, so be still, don't interrupt, and don't ask questions. Are you listening? Well, then. There was once a snake, and he lived in a gooseberry bush, and every night he turned into a handsome prince. Now there is nothing extraordinary about this, it happens all the time, especially in Burma where everyone is handsome anyway... But a story can't succeed unless there's a woman in it, so there was also a woman who lived in a little bamboo house with orchids hanging in the verandah, and she had three daughters called Ma Gyi, Ma Lat, and Ma Nge. And Ma Nge was the youngest and the nicest and the most beautiful, because a story can't succeed unless she is all these things.

Well, one day the mother of Ma Nge had to go out to fetch gooseberries from the forest. They were bitter gooseberries: Burmese ladies call them *zi-byu-thi*, and prefer them to sweet gooseberries. And the woman took her basket along; and just as she was starting to pick gooseberries, the snake who lived in the gooseberry bush hissed at her, as much as to say: 'Be off.' This was the snake who was a prince by night, but now of course it was broad daylight, and anyway Burmese women aren't afraid of snakes. Moreover, the snake recalled that this was the mother of three daughters, and he had a fondness for daughters, so he changed his mind about sending the woman away, and waited for her to speak first, because she was a woman, and women are remarkable for their business capacity.

The woman said: 'Please give me a gooseberry.' Women are always wanting something; it's a part of their business philosophy.

But the snake said no. He had remembered that he was a prince and that princes aren't supposed to say yes to anything; not at first, anyway. It was a matter of principle.

Then the woman said: 'If you like my eldest daughter, Ma Gyi, give me a gooseberry.' He didn't care for Ma Gyi, because he knew she had a terrible temper (or perhaps it was a distemper), but he gave the woman a gooseberry as a matter of policy. 'One gooseberry is about all that Ma Gyi's worth,' he said to himself.

But women all over the world, from Burma to Bermuda and beyond, are never satisfied with only *one* of anything, and she said: 'If you like my second daughter, Ma Lat, give me another gooseberry.'

The prince knew that Ma Lat had a squint, but he didn't want to hurt anyone's feelings, so he gave the woman another gooseberry; and thus encouraged, she said: 'And if you like my youngest daughter, Ma Nge, give me another gooseberry.'

At that the snake trembled so violently from tip to tail that every gooseberry fell off the bush; for the snake-prince knew that Ma Nge was the youngest and nicest and most beautiful of them all. And the woman gathered up all the gooseberries, put them in her basket, and took them home because they were bitter (*zi-byu-thi*), and because she was a woman of remarkable business capacity.

On the way she met a signpost and gave it a gooseberry, saying: 'If a snake comes enquiring which way I have gone, don't tell him, but point in the opposite direction.' She said this because she knew the signpost would do just the opposite.

Then she went on and said the same thing to two more signposts (everything has to be done three times in the best stories), and the posts all did the same thing, which was to show the snake the proper road, because that is what signposts are supposed to do.

The snake had little difficulty in following the woman to her house. He hid in a large jar, and when she came to get something, he slid out and coiled round her arm in the manner of a prospective son-in-law.

'If you love my daughter Ma Gyi, let go,' cried the woman, pretending to be frightened. (She knew quite well that the snake was a prince.)

But the snake hung on, because he didn't love Ma Gyi, who had a bad temper and probably distemper too.

'If you love Ma Lat, let go!'

But the snake hung on. Although he, personally, had nothing against squinty-eyed women, he did not relish the prospect of being stared at by one all his life.

And then (because everything must be done three times) the woman cried: 'If you love my daughter Ma Nge, let go!'

The snake fell swooning to the ground. And as night had come on quite suddenly, in the snake's place the mother found the supplicant prince, smitten with love for her youngest daughter. And she wasted no time in getting him married to Ma Nge.

That ought to be that end of the story. But in Burma stories don't end, they just go on and on forever, so that sometimes it is difficult to print them. But the prince had to do something to break the spell, because after some time Ma Nge found it rather irritating being married to a prince who was her husband by night and a snake by day. She said she preferred a man about the place even during the day. It was she who managed to break the spell because, like her mother, she had this remarkable business capacity. All she did was to find her husband a job of work, and the shock was so great that it broke the spell. It was the first time in his life that the prince had been expected to do any work, and he was so shaken that he completely forgot how to turn himself back into a snake. But the prince stuck to his job, and worked so hard that sometimes his wife felt quite lonely; she didn't know that his employers had given him a beautiful secretary, and that this was encouraging him to work overtime. And so, when he came home late and went straight to bed after dinner, she began to scold him and complain of his indifference. One morning he became so disgusted with her constant nagging that he found he could remember the magic spell and immediately turned himself into an enormous snake.

He started by trying to swallow his wife's feet. Ma Nge called out to her mother, but her mother said that was quite all right.

'He has swallowed my knees,' sailed poor Ma Nge.

'Never mind, dear,' replied her mother, who was cooking in the next room. 'You never can tell what an amorous husband will do.'

'He has swallowed my neck.'

The mother thought this was going too far; and when no further calls came from her daughter, she burst into the room and remonstrated with the snake, who had entirely swallowed Ma Nge.

'Give her up at once,' cried the indignant mother.

'Not unless you agree to may terms.' said the snake. 'First, I'm to be a snake whenever I feel like it. Second, I'm to be a real prince and go to work only when I feel like it. How can your daughter love me if I come home tired from the office like any other man? You wanted a prince for a son-in-law. You got one. Now you must let me live like a prince.'

The mother agreed to his terms, and he unswallowed his wife, and from that day onwards the two women did all the work while the prince sat in the verandah under the hanging orchids and drank a wonderful beer made from bitter gooseberries.

Escape from Java

'No one, it seemed, was interested in defending Java, only in getting out as fast as possible.'

It all happened within the space of a few days. The cassia tree had barely come into flower when the first bombs fell on Batavia (now called Jakarta) and the bright pink blossoms lay scattered over the wreckage in the streets.

News had reached us that Singapore had fallen to the Japanese. My father said: 'I expect it won't be long before they take Java. With the British defeated, how can the Dutch be expected to win!' He did not mean to be critical of the Dutch; he knew they did not have the backing of an Empire such as Britain then had. Singapore had been called the Gibraltar of the East. After its surrender there could only be retreat, a vast exodus of Europeans from South-East Asia.

It was World War II. What the Javanese thought about the war is now hard for me to say, because I was only nine at the time and knew little of worldly matters. Most people knew they would be exchanging their Dutch rulers for Japanese rulers; but there were also many who spoke in terms of freedom for Java when the war was over.

Our neighbor, Mr Hartono, was one of those who looked ahead to a time when Java, Sumatra, and the other islands would make up one independent nation. He was a college professor and spoke Dutch, Chinese, Javanese and a little English. His son, Sono, was about my age. He was the only boy I knew who could talk to me in English, and as a result we spent a lot of time together. Our favourite pastime was flying kites in the park.

The bombing soon put an end to kite flying. Air raid alerts sounded at all hours of the day and night, and although in the beginning most of the bombs fell near the docks, a couple of miles from where we lived, we had to stay indoors. If the planes sounded very near, we dived under beds or tables. I don't remember if there were any trenches. Probably there hadn't been time for trench digging, and now there was time only for digging graves. Events had moved all too swiftly, and everyone (except of course the Javanese) was anxious to get away from Java.

'When are you going?' asked Sono, as we sat on the veranda steps in a pause between air raids.

'I don't know,' I said. 'It all depends on my father,'

'My father says the Japs will be here in a week. And if you're still here then, they'll put you to work building a railway.'

'I wouldn't mind building a railway,' I said.

'But they won't give you enough to eat. Just rice with worms in it. And if you don't work properly they'll shoot you.'

'They do that to soldiers,' I said. 'We're civilians.'

'They do it to civilians, too,' said Sono.

What were my father and I doing in Batavia, when our home had been first in India and then in Singapore? He worked for a firm dealing in rubber, and six months earlier he had been sent to Batavia to open a new office in partnership with a Dutch business house. Although I was so young, I accompanied my father almost everywhere. My mother had died when I was very small, and my father had always looked after me. After the war was over he was going to take me to England.

'Are we going to win the war?' I asked.

'It doesn't look it from here,' he said.

No, it didn't look as though we were winning. Standing at the docks with my father, I watched the ships arrive from Singapore, crowded with refugees—men, women and children all living on the decks in the hot tropical sun; they looked pale and worn-out and worried. They were on their way to Colombo or Bombay. No one came ashore at Batavia. It wasn't British territory; it was Dutch, and everyone knew it wouldn't be Dutch for long.

'Aren't we going too?' I asked. 'Sono's father says the Japs will be here any day.'

'We've still got a few days,' said my father. He was a short, stocky man, who seldom got excited. If he was worried, he didn't show it. 'I've got to wind up a few business matters, and then we'll be off.'

'How will we go? There's no room for us on those ships.'

'There certainly isn't. But we'll find a way, lad, don't worry.'

I didn't worry. I had complete confidence in my father's ability to find a way out of difficulties. He used to say, 'Every problem has a solution hidden away somewhere, and if only you look hard enough enough you will find it.

There were British soldiers in the streets but they did not make us feel much safer. They were just waiting for troop ships to come and take them away. No one, it seemed, was interested in defending Java, only in getting out as fast as possible.

Although the Dutch were unpopular with the Javanese people, there was no ill-feeling against individual Europeans. I could walk safely through the streets. Occasionally small boys in the crowded Chinese quarter would point at me and shout, '*Orang Balandi!*' (Dutchman!) but they did so in good humour, and I didn't know the language well enough to stop and explain that the English weren't Dutch. For them, all white people were the same, and understandably so.

My father's office was in the commercial area, along the canal banks. Our two-storied house, about a mile away, was an old building with a roof of red tiles and a broad balcony which had stone dragons at either end. There were flowers in the garden almost all the year round. If there was anything in Batavia more regular than the bombing, it was the rain, which came pattering down on the roof and on the banana fronds almost every afternoon. In the hot and steamy atmosphere of Java, the rain was always welcome.

There were no anti-aircraft guns in Batavia—at least we never heard any—and the Jap bombers came over at will, dropping their bombs by daylight. Sometimes bombs fell in the town. One day the building next to my father's office received a direct hit and tumbled into the river. A number of office workers were killed.

One day Sono said, 'The bombs are falling on Batavia, not in the countryside. Why don't we get cycles and ride out of town?'

I fell in with the idea at once. After the morning all-clear had sounded, we mounted our cycles and rode out of town. Mine was a hired cycle, but Sono's was his own. He'd had it since the age of five, and it was constantly in need of repairs. 'The soul has gone out of it,' he used to say.

Our fathers were at work; Sono's mother had gone out to do her shopping (during air-raids she took shelter under the most convenient shop-counter) and wouldn't be back for at least an hour. We expected to be back before lunch.

We were soon out of town, on a road that passed through rice fields, pineapple orchards and cinchona plantations. On our right lay dark green hills; on our left, groves of coconut palms, and beyond them, the sea. Men and women were working in the rice fields, knee-deep in mud, their broad-brimmed hats protecting them from the fierce sun. Here and there a buffalo wallowed in a pool of brown water, while a naked boy lay stretched out on the animal's broad back.

We took a bumpy track through the palms. They grew right down to the edge of the sea. Leaving our cycles on the shingle, we ran down a smooth, sandy beach and into the shallow water.

'Don't go too far in,' warned Sono. 'There may be sharks about.'

Wading in amongst the rocks, we searched for interesting shells, then sat down on a large rock and looked out to sea, where a sailing ship moved placidly on the crisp blue waters. It was difficult to imagine that half the world was at war, and that Batavia, two or three miles away, was right in the middle of it.

On our way home we decided to take a short cut through the rice fields, but soon found that our tires got bogged down in the soft mud. This delayed our return; and to make things worse, we got the roads mixed up and reached an area of the town that seemed unfamiliar. We had barely entered the outskirts when the siren sounded, to be followed soon after by the drone of approaching aircraft.

'Should we get off our cycles and take shelter somewhere?' I called out.

'No, let's race home!' shouted Sono. 'The bombs won't fall here.'

But he was wrong. The planes flew in very low. Looking up for a moment, I saw the sun blotted out by the sinister shape of a Jap fighter-bomber. We pedalled furiously; but we had barely covered fifty yards when there was a terrific explosion on our right, behind some houses. The shock sent us spinning across the road. We were flung from our cycles. And the cycles, still propelled by the blast, crashed into a wall.

I felt a stinging sensation in my hands and legs, as though scores of little insects had bitten me. Tiny droplets of blood appeared here and there on my flesh. Sono was on all fours, crawling beside me, and I saw that he too had the same small scratches on his hands and forehead, made by tiny shards of flying glass.

We were quickly on our feet, and then we began running in the general direction of our homes. The twisted cycles lay forgotten in the road.

'Get off the street, you two!' shouted someone from a window; but we weren't going to stop running until we got home. And we ran faster than we'd ever run in our lives.

My father and Sono's parents were themselves running about the street, calling for us, when we came rushing around the corner and tumbled into their arms.

'Where have you been?'

'What happened to you?'

'How did you get those cuts?'

All superfluous questions; but before we could recover our breath and start explaining, we were bundled into our respective homes. My father washed my cuts and scratches, dabbed at my face and legs with iodine—ignoring my yelps—and then stuck plaster all over my face.

Sono and I had both had a fright, and we did not venture far from the house again.

That night my father said: 'I think we'll able to leave in a day or two.'

'Has another ship come in?'

'No.'

'Then how are we going? By plane?'

'Wait and see, lad. It isn't settled yet. But we won't be able to take much with us—just enough to fill a couple of travelling bags.'

'What about the stamp collection?' I asked.

My father's stamp collection was quite valuable, and filled several volumes.

'I'm afraid we'll have to leave most of it behind,' he said. 'Perhaps Mr Hartono will keep it for me, and when the war is over—if it's ever over—we'll come back for it.'

'But we can take one or two albums with us, can't we?'

'I'll take one. There'll be room for one. Then if we're short of money in Bombay, we can sell the stamps.'

'Bombay? That's in India. I thought we were going back to England.'

'First we must go to India.'

The following morning I found Sono in the garden, patched up like me, and with one foot in a bandage. But he was as cheerful as ever and gave me his usual wide grin.

'We're leaving tomorrow,' I said.

The grin left his face.

'I will be sad when you go,' he said. 'But I will be glad too, because then you will be able to escape from the Japs.'

'After the war, I'll come back.'

'Yes, you must come back. And then, when we are big, we will go round the world together. I want to see England and America and Africa and India and Japan. I want to go everywhere.'

'We can't go everywhere.'

'Yes, we can. No one can stop us!'

We had to be up very early the next morning. Our bags had been packed late at night. We were taking a few clothes, some of my father's business papers, a pair of binoculars, one stamp album, and several bars of chocolate. I was pleased about the stamp album and the chocolates, but I had to give up several of my treasures—favourite books, the gramophone and records, an old Samurai sword, a train set and a dartboard. The only consolation was that Sono, and not a stranger, would have them.

In the first faint light of dawn a truck drew up in front of the house. It was driven by a Dutch businessman, Mr Hookens, who worked with my father. Sono was already at the gate, waiting to say good-bye.

'I have a present for you,' he said.

He took me by the hand and pressed a smooth, hard object into my palm. I grasped it and then held it up against the light. It was a beautiful little sea horse, carved out of pale blue jade.

'It will bring you luck,' said Sono.

'Thank you,' I said. 'I will keep it forever.'

And I slipped the little sea horse into my pocket.

'In you get, lad,' said my father, and I got up on the front seat between him and Mr Hookens.

As the truck started up, I turned to wave to Sono. He was sitting on his garden wall, grinning at me. He called out: 'We will go everywhere, and no one can stop us!'

He was still waving when the truck took us round the bend at the end of the road.

We drove through the still, quiet streets of Batavia, occasionally passing burnt-out trucks and shattered buildings. Then we left the sleeping city far behind and were climbing into the forested hills. It had rained during the night, and when the sun came up over the green hills, it twinkled and glittered on the broad wet leaves. The light in the forest changed from dark green to greenish gold, broken here and there by the flaming red or orange of a trumpet-shaped blossom. It was impossible to know the names of all those fantastic plants! The road had been cut through dense tropical forest, and on either side, the trees jostled each other, hungry for the sun; but they were chained together by the liana creepers and vines that fed upon the same struggling trees.

Occasionally a Jelarang, a large Javan squirrel, frightened by the passing of the truck, leapt through the trees before disappearing into the depths of the forest. We saw many birds: peacocks, jungle-fowl, and once, standing majestically at the side of the road, a crowned pigeon, its great size and splendid crest making it a striking object even at a distance. Mr Hookens slowed down so that we could look at the bird. It bowed its head so that its crest swept the ground; then it emitted a low hollow boom rather than the call of a turkey.

When we came to a small clearing, we stopped for breakfast. Butterflies—black, green and gold—flitted across the clearing. The silence of the forest was broken only by the drone of airplanes, Japanese Zeros heading for Batavia on another raid. I thought about Sono, and wondered what he would be doing at home: probably trying out the gramophone!

We ate boiled eggs and drank tea from a thermos, then got back into the truck and resumed our journey.

I must have dozed off soon after because the next thing I remember is that we were going quite fast down a steep, winding road, and in the distance I could see a calm blue lagoon.

'We've reached the sea again,' I said.

'That's right,' said my father. 'But we're now nearly a hundred miles from Batavia, in another part of the island. You're looking out over the Sunda Straits.'

Then he pointed towards a shimmering white object resting on the waters of the lagoon.

'There's our plane,' he said.

'A seaplane!' I exclaimed. 'I never guessed. Where will it take us?'

'To India, I hope. There aren't many other places left to go to!'

It was a very old seaplane, and no one, not even the captain—the pilot was called the captain—could promise that it would take off. Mr Hookens wasn't coming with us; he said the plane would be back for him the next day. Besides my father and me, there were four other passengers, and all but one were Dutch. The odd man out was a Londoner, a motor mechanic who'd been left behind in Java when his unit was evacuated. (He told us later that he'd fallen asleep at a bar in the Chinese quarter, waking up some hours after his regiment had moved off!) He looked rather scruffy. He'd lost the top button of his shirt, but instead of leaving his collar open, as we did, he'd kept it together with a large safety pin, which thrust itself out from behind a bright pink tie.

'It's a relief to find you here, guvnor,' he said, shaking my father by the hand. 'Knew you for a Yorkshireman the minute I set eyes on you. It's the *song-fried* that does it, if you know what I mean.' (He meant *sang-froid*, French for a 'cool look'.) 'And here I was, with all these flippin' forriners, and me not knowing a word of what they've been yattering about. Do you think this old tub will get us back to Blighty?'

'It does look a bit shaky,' said my father. 'One of the first flying boats, from the looks of it. If it gets us to Bombay, that's far enough.'

'Anywhere out of Java's good enough for me,' said our new companion. 'The name's Muggeridge.'

'Pleased to know you, Mr Muggeridge,' said my father, 'I'm Bond. This is my son.'

Mr Muggeridge rumpled my hair and favoured me with a large wink.

The captain of the seaplane was beckoning to us to join him in a small skiff which was about to take us across a short stretch of water to the seaplane.

'Here we go,' said Mr Muggeridge. 'Say your prayers and keep your fingers crossed.'

The seaplane was a long time getting airborne. It had to make several runs before it finally took off; then, lurching drunkenly, it rose into the clear blue sky.

'For a moment I thought we were going to end up in the briny,' said Mr Muggeridge, untying his seat belt, 'And talkin' of fish, I'd give a week's wages for a plate of fish an' chips and a pint of beer.'

'I'll buy you a beer in Calcutta,' said my father.

'Have an egg,' I said, remembering we still had some boiled eggs in one of the travelling bags.

'Thanks, mate,' said Mr Muggeridge, accepting an egg with alacrity. 'A real egg, too! I've been livin' on egg powder these last six months. That's what they give you in the Army. And it ain't hens' eggs they make it from, let me tell you. It's either gulls' or turtles' eggs!'

'No,' said my father with a straight face. 'Snakes' eggs.'

Mr Muggeridge turned a delicate shade of green; but he soon recovered his poise, and for about an hour kept talking about almost everything under the sun, including Churchill, Hitler, Roosevelt, Mahatma Gandhi and Betty Grable. (The last-named was famous for her beautiful legs.) He would have gone on talking all the way to India had he been given a chance; but suddenly a shudder passed through the old plane, and it began lurching again.

'I think an engine is giving trouble,' said my father.

When I looked through the small glassed-in window, it seemed as though the sea was rushing up to meet us.

The co-pilot entered the passenger cabin and said something in Dutch. The passengers looked dismayed, and immediately began fastening their seat belts.

'Well, what did the blighter say?' asked Mr Muggeridge.

'I think he's going to have to ditch the plane,' said my father, who knew enough Dutch to get the gist of anything that was said.

'Down in the drink!' exclaimed Mr Muggeridge. 'Gawd 'elp us! And how far are we from India, guv?'

A few hundred miles,' said my father.

'Can you swim, mate?' asked Mr Muggeridge looking at me.

'Yes,' I said. 'But not all the way to Bombay. How far can you swim?'

'The length of a bathtub,' he said.

'Don't worry,' said my father. 'Just make sure your life jacket's properly tied.'

We looked to our life jackets; my father checked mine twice, making sure that it was properly fastened.

The pilot had now cut both engines, and was bringing the plane down in a circling movement. But he couldn't control the speed, and it was tilting heavily to one side. Instead of landing smoothly on its belly, it came down on a wing tip, and this caused the plane to swivel violently around in the choppy sea. There was a terrific jolt when the plane hit the water, and if it hadn't been for the seat belts, we'd have been flung from our seats. Even so, Mr Muggeridge struck his head against the seat in front, and he was now holding a bleeding nose and using some shocking language.

As soon as the plane came to a standstill, my father undid my seat belt. There was no time to lose. Water was already filling the cabin, and all the passengers—except one, who was dead in his seat with a broken neck—were scrambling for the exit hatch. The co-pilot pulled a lever and the door fell away to reveal high waves slapping against the sides of the stricken plane.

Holding me by the hand, my father was leading me towards the exit.

'Quick lad,' he said. 'We won't stay afloat for long.'

'Give us a hand!' shouted Mr Muggeridge, still struggling with his life jacket. 'First this bloody bleedin' nose, and now something's gone and stuck.'

My father helped him fix the life jacket, then pushed him out of the door ahead of us.

As we swam away from the seaplane (Mr Muggeridge splashing furiously alongside us), we were aware of the other passengers in the water. One of them shouted to us in Dutch to follow him.

We swam after him towards the dinghy, which had been released the moment we hit the water. That yellow dinghy, bobbing about on the waves, was as welcome as land.

All who had left the plane managed to climb into the dinghy. We were seven altogether—a tight fit. We had hardly settled down in the well of the dinghy when Mr Muggeridge, still holding his nose, exclaimed: 'There she goes!' And as we looked on helplessly, the seaplane sank swiftly and silently beneath the waves.

The dinghy had shipped a lot of water, and soon everyone was busy bailing it out with mugs (there were a couple in the dinghy), hats, and bare hands. There was a light swell, and every now and then water would roll in again and half fill the dinghy. But within half an hour we had most of the water out, and then it was possible to take turns, two men doing the bailing while the others rested. No one expected me to do this work, but I took a hand anyway, using my father's sola-topee for the purpose.

'Where are we?' asked one of the passengers.

'A long way from anywhere,' said another.

'There must be a few islands in the Indian Ocean.'

'But we may be at sea for days before we come to one of them.'

'Days or even weeks,' said the captain. 'Let us look at our supplies.'

The dinghy appeared to be fairly well provided with emergency rations: biscuits, raisins, chocolates (we'd lost our own), and enough water to last a week. There was also a first-aid box, which was put to immediate use, as Mr Muggeridge's nose needed attention. A few others had cuts and bruises. One of the passengers had received a hard knock on the head and appeared to be suffering from loss of memory. He had no idea how we happened to be drifting about in the middle of the Indian Ocean; he was convinced that we were on a pleasure cruise a few miles off Batavia.

The unfamiliar motion of the dinghy, as it rose and fell in the troughs between the waves, resulted in almost everyone getting seasick. As no one could eat anything, a day's rations were saved.

The sun was very hot, but my father covered my head with a large spotted handkerchief. He'd always had a fancy for bandana handkerchiefs with yellow spots, and seldom carried fewer than two on his person; so he had one for himself too. The sola-topee, well soaked in seawater, was being used by Mr Muggeridge.

It was only when I had recovered to some extent from my seasickness that I remembered the valuable stamp album, and sat up, exclaiming, 'The stamps! Did you bring the stamp album, Dad?'

He shook his head ruefully. 'It must be at the bottom of the sea by now,' he said. 'But don't worry, I kept a few rare stamps in my wallet.' And looking pleased with himself, he tapped the pocket of his bush shirt.

The dinghy drifted all day, with no one having the least idea where it might be taking us.

'Probably going round in circles,' said Mr Muggeridge pessimistically.

There was no compass and no sail, and paddling wouldn't have got us far even if we'd had paddles; we could only resign ourselves to the whims of the current and hope it would take us towards land or at least to within hailing distance of some passing ship.

The sun went down like an overripe tomato dissolving slowly in the sea. The darkness pressed down on us. It was a moonless night, and all we could see was the white foam on the crests of the waves. I lay with my head on my father's shoulder, and looked up at the stars which glittered in the remote heavens.

'Perhaps your friend Sono will look up at the sky tonight and see those same stars,' said my father. 'The world isn't so big after all.'

'All the same, there's a lot of sea around us,' said Mr Muggeridge from out of the darkness.

Remembering Sono, I put my hand in my pocket and was reassured to feel the smooth outline of the jade seahorse.

'I've still got Sono's seahorse,' I said, showing it to my father.

'Keep it carefully,' he said. 'It may bring us luck.'

'Are seahorses lucky?'

'Who knows? But he gave it to you with love, and love is like a prayer. So keep it carefully.'

I didn't sleep much that night. I don't think anyone slept. No one spoke much either, except of course Mr Muggeridge, who kept muttering something about cold beer and salami.

I didn't feel so sick the next day. By ten o'clock I was quite hungry; but breakfast consisted of two biscuits, a piece of chocolate, and a little drinking water. It was another hot day, and we were soon very thirsty, but everyone agreed that we should ration ourselves strictly.

Two or three still felt ill, but the others, including Mr Muggeridge, had recovered their appetites and normal spirits, and there was some discussion about the prospects of being picked up.

'Are there any distress-rockets in the dinghy?' asked my father. 'If we see a ship or a plane, we can fire a rocket and hope to be spotted. Otherwise there's not much chance of our being seen from a distance.'

A thorough search was made in the dinghy, but there were no rockets.

'Someone must have used them last Guy Fawkes Day,' commented Mr Muggeridge.

'They don't celebrate Guy Fawkes Day in Holland,' said my father. 'Guy Fawkes was an Englishman.'

'Ah,' said Mr Muggeridge, not in the least put out. 'I've always said, most great men are Englishmen. And what did this chap Guy Fawkes do?'

'Tried to blow up Parliament,' said my father.

That afternoon we saw our first sharks. They were enormous creatures, and as they glided backward and forward under the boat it seemed they might hit and capsize us. They went away for some time, but returned in the evening.

At night, as I lay half asleep beside my father, I felt a few drops of water strike my face. At first I thought it was the seaspray; but when the sprinkling continued, I realised that it was raining lightly.

'Rain!' I shouted, sitting up. 'It's raining!'

Everyone woke up and did their best to collect water in mugs, hats or other containers. Mr Muggeridge lay back with his mouth open, drinking the rain as it fell.

'This is more like it,' he said. 'You can have all the sun an' sand in the world. Give me a rainy day in England!'

But by early morning the clouds had passed, and the day turned out to be even hotter than the previous one. Soon we were all red and raw from sunburn. By midday even

Mr Muggeridge was silent. No one had the energy to talk.

Then my father whispered, 'Can you hear a plane, lad?'

I listened carefully, and above the hiss of the waves I heard what sounded like the distant drone of a plane; but it must have been very far away, because we could not see it. Perhaps it was flying into the sun, and the glare was too much for our sore eyes; or perhaps we'd just imagined the sound.

Then the Dutchman who'd lost his memory thought he saw land, and kept pointing towards the horizon and saying, 'That's Batavia, I told you we were close to shore!' No one else saw anything. So my father and I weren't the only ones imagining things.

Said my father, 'It only goes to show that a man can see what he wants to see, even if there's nothing to be seen!

The sharks were still with us. Mr Muggeridge began to resent them. He took off one of his shoes and hurled it at the nearest shark; but the big fish ignored the shoe and swam on after us.

'Now, if your leg had been in that shoe, Mr Muggeridge, the shark might have accepted it,' observed my father.

'Don't throw your shoes away,' said the captain. 'We might land on a deserted coastline and have to walk hundreds of miles!'

A light breeze sprang up that evening, and the dinghy moved more swiftly on the choppy water.

'At last we're moving forward,' said the captain.

'In circles,' said Mr Muggeridge.

But the breeze was refreshing; it cooled our burning limbs and helped us to get some sleep. In the middle of the night I woke up feeling very hungry.

'Are you all right?' asked my father, who had been awake all the time.

'Just hungry,' I said.

'And what would you like to eat?'

'Oranges!'

He laughed. 'No oranges on board. But I kept a piece of my chocolate for you. And there's a little water, if you're thirsty.'

I kept the chocolate in my mouth for a long time, trying to make it last. Then I sipped a little water.

'Aren't you hungry?' I asked.

'Ravenous! I could eat a whole turkey. When we get to Calcutta or Madras or Colombo, or wherever it is we get to, we'll go to the best restaurant in town and eat like—like—'

'Like shipwrecked sailors!' I said.

'Exactly.'

'Do you think we'll ever get to land Dad?'

'I'm sure we will. You're not afraid, are you?'

'No. Not as long as you're with me.'

Next morning, to everyone's delight, we saw seagulls. This was a sure sign that land couldn't be far away; but a dinghy could take days to drift a distance of thirty or forty miles. The birds wheeled noisily above the dinghy. Their cries were the first familiar sounds we had heard for three days and three nights, apart from the wind and the sea and our own weary voices.

The sharks had disappeared, and that too was an encouraging sign. They didn't like the oil slicks that were appearing in the water.

But presently the gulls left us, and we feared we were drifting away from land.

'Circles,' repeated Mr Muggeridge. 'Circles.'

We had sufficient food and water for another week at sea; but no one even wanted to think about spending another week at sea.

The sun was a ball of fire. Our water ration wasn't sufficient to quench our thirst. By noon we were without much hope or energy.

My father had his pipe in his mouth. He didn't have any tobacco, but he liked holding the pipe between his teeth. He said it prevented his mouth from getting too dry.

The sharks came back.

Mr Muggeridge removed his other shoe and threw it at them.

'Nothing like a lovely wet English summer,' he mumbled.

I fell asleep in the well of the dinghy, my father's large handkerchief spread over my face. The yellow spots on the cloth seemed to grow into enormous revolving suns.

When I woke up, I found a huge shadow hanging over us. At first I thought it was a cloud. But it was a shifting shadow. My father took the handkerchief from my face and said, 'You can wake up now, lad. We'll be home and dry soon.'

A fishing boat was beside us, and the shadow came from its wide flapping sail. A number of bronzed, smiling, chattering fishermen—Burmese, as we discovered later—were gazing down at us from the deck of their boat.

A few days later my father and I were in Calcutta.

My father sold his rare stamps for over a thousand rupees, and we were able to live in a comfortable hotel. Mr Muggeridge was flown back to England. Later we got a postcard from him, saying the English rain was awful!

'And what about us?' I asked. 'Aren't we going back to England?'

'Not yet,' said my father. 'You'll be going to a boarding school in Simla, until the war's over.'

'But why should I leave you?' I asked.

'Because I've joined the R.A.F.,' he said. 'Don't worry, I'm being posted in Delhi. I'll be able to come up to see you sometimes.'

A week later I was on a small train which went chugging up the steep mountain track to Simla. Several Indian, Ango-Indian and English children tumbled around in the compartment. I felt quite out of place among them, as though I had grown out of their pranks. But I wasn't unhappy. I knew my father would be coming to see me soon. He'd promised me some books, a pair of rollerskates, and a cricket bat, just as soon as he got his first month's pay.

Meanwhile, I had the jade seahorse which Sono had given me.

And I have it with me today.

The Girl on the Train

I had the train compartment to myself up to Rohana, then a girl got in. The couple who saw her off were probably her parents; they seemed very anxious about her comfort, and the woman gave the girl detailed instructions as to where to keep her things, when not to lean out of windows, and how to avoid speaking to strangers.

They called their goodbyes and the train pulled out of the station. As I was going blind at the time, my eyes sensitive only to light and darkness, I was unable to tell what the girl looked like; but I knew she wore slippers from the way they slapped against her heels.

It would take me some time to discover something about her looks, and perhaps I never would. But I liked the sound of her voice, and even the sound of her slippers.

'Are you going all the way to Dehra?' I asked.

I must have been sitting in a dark corner, because my voice startled her. She gave a little exclamation and said, 'I didn't know anyone else was here.'

Well, it often happens that people with good eyesight fail to see what is right in front of them. They have too much to take in, I suppose. Whereas people who cannot see (or see very little) have to take in only the essentials, whatever registers most tellingly on their remaining senses.

'I didn't see you either,' I said. 'But I heard you come in.'

I wondered if I would be able to prevent her from discovering that I was blind. Provided I keep to my seat, I thought, it shouldn't be too difficult.

The girl said, 'I'm getting off at Saharanpur. My aunt is meeting me there.'

Then I had better not get too familiar,' I replied. 'Aunts are usually formidable creatures.'

'Where are you going?' she asked.

'To Dehra, and then to Mussoorie.'

'Oh, how lucky you are. I wish I were going to Mussoorie. I love the hills. Especially in October.'

'Yes, this is the best time,' I said, calling on my memories. 'The hills are covered with wild dahlias, the sun is delicious, and at night you can sit in front of a logfire and drink a little brandy. Most of the tourists have gone, and the roads are quiet and almost deserted. Yes, October is the best time.'

She was silent. I wondered if my words had touched her, or whether she thought me a romantic fool. Then I made a mistake.

'What is it like outside?' I asked.

She seemed to find nothing strange in the question. Had she noticed already that I could not see? But her next question removed my doubts.

'Why don't you look out of the window?' she asked.

I moved easily along the berth and felt for the window ledge. The window was open, and I faced it, making a pretence of studying the landscape. I heard the panting of the engine, the rumble of the wheels, and, in my mind's eye, I could see telegraph posts flashing by.

'Have you noticed,' I ventured, 'that the trees seem to be moving while we seem to be standing still?'

'That always happens,' she said. 'Do you see any animals?'

'No,' I answered quite confidently. I knew that there were hardly any animals left in the forests near Dehra.

I turned from the window and faced the girl, and for a while we sat in silence.

'You have an interesting face,' I remarked. I was becoming quite daring, but it was a safe remark. Few girls can resist flattery. She laughed pleasantly—a clear ringing laugh.

'It's nice to be told I have an interesting face. I'm tired of people telling me I have a pretty face.'

Oh, so you do have a pretty face, thought I; and aloud I said, 'Well, an interesting face can also be pretty.'

'You are a very gallant young man,' she said 'but why are you so serious?'

I thought, then, I would try to laugh for her, but the thought of laughter only made me feel troubled and lonely.

'We'll soon be at your station,' I said.

'Thank goodness it's a short journey. I can't bear to sit in a train for more than two or three hours.'

Yet I was prepared to sit there for almost any length of time, just to listen to her talking. Her voice had the sparkle of a mountain stream. As soon as she left the train, she would forget our brief encounter; but it would stay with me for the rest of the journey, and for some time after.

The engine's whistle shrieked, the carriage wheels changed their sound and rhythm, the girl got up and began to collect her things. I wondered if she wore her hair in a bun, or if it was plaited; perhaps it was hanging loose over her shoulders, or was it cut very short?

The train drew slowly into the station. Outside, there was the shouting of porters and vendors and a high-pitched female voice near the carriage door; that voice must have belonged to the girl's aunt.

'Goodbye,' the girl said.

She was standing very close to me, so close that the perfume from her hair was tantalising. I wanted to raise my hand and touch her hair, but she moved away. Only the scent of perfume still lingered where she had stood.

There was some confusion in the doorway. A man, getting into the compartment, stammered an apology. Then the door banged, and the world was shut out again. I returned to my berth. The guard blew his whistle and we moved off. Once again, I had a game to play and a new fellow-traveller.

The train gathered speed, the wheels took up their song, the carriage groaned and shook. I found the window and sat in front of it, staring into the daylight that was darkness for me.

So many things were happening outside the window: it could be a fascinating game, guessing what went on out there.

The man who had entered the compartment broke into my reverie.

'You must be disappointed,' he said. 'I'm not nearly as attractive a travelling companion as the one who just left.'

'She was an interesting girl,' I said. 'Can you tell me—did she keep her hair long or short?'

'I don't remember,' he said, sounding puzzled. 'It was her eyes I noticed, not her hair. She had beautiful eyes—but they were of no use to her. She was completely blind. Didn't you notice?'

He Said it with Arsenic

Is there such a person as a born murderer—in the sense that there are born writers and musicians, born winners and losers?

One can't be sure. The urge to do away with troublesome people is common to most of us, but only a few succumb to it.

If ever there was a born murderer, he must surely have been William Jones. The thing came so naturally to him. No extreme violence, no messy shootings or hackings or throttling; just the right amount of poison, administered with skill and discretion.

A gentle, civilised sort of person was Mr Jones. He collected butterflies and arranged them systematically in glass cases. His ether bottle was quick and painless. He never stuck pins into the beautiful creatures.

Have you ever heard of the Agra Double Murder? It happened, of course, a great many years ago, when Agra was a far-flung outpost of the British Empire. In those days, William Jones was a male nurse in one of the city's hospitals. The patients—especially terminal cases—spoke highly of the care and consideration he showed them. While most nurses, both male and female, preferred to attend to the more hopeful cases, nurse William was always prepared to stand duty over a dying patient.

He felt a certain empathy for the dying; he liked to see them on their way. It was just his good nature, of course.

On a visit to nearby Meerut, he met and fell in love with Mrs Browning, the wife of the local station-master. Impassioned love letters were soon putting a strain on the Agra-Meerut postal service. The envelopes grew heavier—not so much because the letters were growing longer but because they contained little packets of a powdery white substance, accompanied by detailed instructions as to its correct administration.

Mr Browning, an unassuming and trustful man—one of the world's born losers, in fact—was not the sort to read his wife's correspondence. Even when he was seized by frequent attacks of colic, he put them down to an impure water supply. He recovered from one bout of vomitting and diarrhoea only to be racked by another.

He was hospitalised on a diagnosis of gastroenteritis; and, thus freed from his wife's ministrations, soon got better. But on returning home and drinking a glass of nimbu-pani brought to him by the solicitous Mrs Browning, he had a relapse from which he did not recover.

Those were the days when deaths from cholera and related diseases were only too common in India, and death certificates were easier to obtain than dog licences.

After a short interval of mourning (it was the hot weather and you couldn't wear black for long), Mrs Browning moved to Agra, where she rented a house next door to William Jones.

I forgot to mention that Mr Jones was also married. His wife was an insignificant creature, no match for a genius like William. Before the hot weather was over, the dreaded cholera had taken her too. The way was clear for the lovers to unite in holy matrimony.

But Dame Gossip lived in Agra too, and it was not long before tongues were wagging and anonymous letters were being received by the Superintendent of Police. Enquiries were instituted. Like most infatuated lovers, Mrs Browning had hung on to her beloved's letters and billet-doux, and these soon came to light. The silly woman had kept them in a box beneath her bed.

Exhumations were ordered in both Agra and Meerut.

Arsenic keeps well, even in the hottest of weather, and there was no dearth of it in the remains of both the victims.

Mr Jones and Mrs Browning were arrested and charged with murder.

'Is Uncle Bill really a murderer?' I asked from the drawing room sofa in my grandmother's house in Dehra. (It's time that I told you that William Jones was my uncle, my mother's half-brother.)

I was eight or nine at the time. Uncle Bill had spent the previous summer with us in Dehra and had stuffed me with bazaar sweets and pastries, all of which I had consumed without suffering any ill effects.

'Who told you that about Uncle Bill?' asked Grandmother.

'I heard it in school. All the boys were asking me the same question—"Is your uncle a murderer?" They say he poisoned both his wives.'

'He had only one wife,' snapped Aunt Mabel.

'Did he poison her?'

'No, of course not. How can you say such a thing!'

'Then why is Uncle Bill in gaol?'

'Who says he's in gaol?'

'The boys at school. They heard it from their parents. Uncle Bill is to go on trial in the Agra fort.'

There was a pregnant silence in the drawing room, then Aunt Mabel burst out: 'It was all that awful woman's fault.'

'Do you mean Mrs Browning?' asked Grandmother.

'Yes, of course. She must have put him up to it. Bill couldn't have thought of anything so—so diabolical!'

'But he sent her the powders, dear. And don't forget—Mrs Browning has since....'

Grandmother stopped in mid-sentence, and both she and Aunt Mabel glanced surreptitiously at me.

'Committed suicide,' I filled in. 'There were still some powders with her.'

Aunt Mabel's eyes rolled heavenwards. 'This boy is impossible. I don't know what he will be like when he grows up.'

'At least I won't be like Uncle Bill,' I said. 'Fancy poisoning people! If I kill anyone, it will be in a fair fight. I suppose they'll hang Uncle?'

'Oh, I hope not!'

Grandmother was silent. Uncle Bill was her stepson, but she did have a soft spot for him. Aunt Mabel, his sister, thought he was wonderful. I had always considered him to be a bit soft but had to admit that he was generous. I tried to imagine him dangling at the end of a hangman's rope, but somehow he didn't fit the picture.

As things turned out, he wasn't hanged. White people in India seldom got the death sentence, although the hangman was pretty busy disposing off dacoits and political terrorists. Uncle Bill was given a life sentence and settled down to a sedentary job in the prison library at Naini, near Allahabad. His gifts as a male nurse went unappreciated; they did not trust him in the hospital.

He was released after seven or eight years, shortly after the country became an independent Republic. He came out of gaol to find that the British were leaving, either for England or the remaining colonies. Grandmother was dead. Aunt Mabel and her husband had settled in South Africa. Uncle Bill realised that there was little future for him in India and followed his sister out to Johannesburg. I was then in my last year at boarding school. After my father's death, my mother had married an Indian, and now my future lay in India.

I did not see Uncle Bill after his release from prison, and no one dreamt that he would ever turn up again in India.

In fact, fifteen years were to pass before he came back, and by then I was in my early thirties, the author of a book that had become something of a bestseller. The previous fifteen years had been a struggle—the sort of struggle that every young freelance writer experiences—but at last the hard work was paying off and the royalties were beginning to come in.

I was living in a small cottage on the outskirts of the hill-station of Fosterganj, working on another book, when I received an unexpected visitor.

He was a thin, stooping, grey-haired man in his late fifties, with a straggling moustache and discoloured teeth. He looked feeble and harmless but for his eyes which were pale cold blue. There was something slightly familiar about him.

'Don't you remember me? He asked. 'Not that I really expect you to, after all these years....'

'Wait a minute. Did you teach me at school?'

'No—but you're getting warm.' He put his suitcase down and I glimpsed his name on the airlines label. I looked up in astonishment. 'You're not—you couldn't be...'

'Your Uncle Bill,' he said with a grin and extended his hand. 'None other!' And he sauntered into the house.

I must admit that I had mixed feelings about his arrival. While I had never felt any dislike for him, I hadn't exactly approved of what he had done. Poisoning, I felt, was a particularly reprehensible way of getting rid of inconvenient people: not that I could think of any commendable ways of getting rid of them! Still, it had happened a long time ago, he'd been punished, and presumably he was a reformed character.

'And what have you been doing all these years?' he asked me, easing himself into the only comfortable chair in the room.

'Oh just writing,' I said.

'Yes, I heard about your last book. It's quite a success, isn't it?'

'It's doing quite well. Have you read it?'

'I don't do much reading.'

'And what have you been doing all these years, Uncle Bill?'

'Oh, knocking about here and there. Worked for a soft drink company for some time. And then with a drug firm. My knowledge of chemicals was useful.'

'Weren't you with Aunt Mabel in South Africa?'

'I saw quite a lot of her, until she died a couple of years ago. Didn't you know?'

'No. I've been out of touch with relatives.' I hoped he'd take that as a hint. 'And what about her husband?'

'Died too, not long after. Not many of us left, my boy. That's why, when I saw something about you in the papers, I thought—why not go and see my only nephew again?'

'You're welcome to stay a few days,' I said quickly. 'Then I have to go to Bombay.' (This was a lie, but I did not relish the prospect of looking after Uncle Bill for the rest of his days.)

'Oh, I won't be staying long,' he said. 'I've got a bit of money put by in Johannesburg. It's just that—so far as I know—you're my only living relative, and I thought it would be nice to see you again.'

Feeling relieved, I set about trying to make Uncle Bill as comfortable as possible. I gave him my bedroom and turned the window-seat into a bed for myself. I was a hopeless cook but, using all my ingenuity, I scrambled some eggs for supper. He waved aside my apologies; he'd always been a frugal eater, he said. Eight years in gaol had given him a cast-iron stomach.

He did not get in my way but left me to my writing and my lonely walks. He seemed content to sit in the spring sunshine and smoke his pipe.

It was during our third evening together that he said, 'Oh, I almost forgot. There's a bottle of sherry, in my suitcase. I brought it especially for you.'

'That was very thoughtful of you. Uncle Bill. How did you know I was fond of sherry?'

'Just my intuition. You do like it, don't you?'

'There's nothing like a good sherry.'

He went to his bedroom and came back with an unopened bottle of South African sherry.

'Now you just relax near the fire,' he said agreeably. 'I'll open the bottle and fetch glasses.'

He went to the kitchen while I remained near the electric fire, flipping through some journals. It seemed to me that Uncle Bill was taking rather a long time. Intuition must be a family trait, because it came to me quite suddenly—the thought that Uncle Bill might be intending to poison me.

After all, I thought, here he is after nearly fifteen years, apparently for purely sentimental reasons. But I had just published a bestseller. And I was his nearest relative. If I was to die, Uncle Bill could lay claim to my estate and probably live comfortably on my royalties for the next five or six years!

What had really happened to Aunt Mabel and her husband, I wondered. And where did Uncle Bill get the money for an air ticket to India?

Before I could ask myself any more questions, he reappeared with the glasses on a tray. He set the tray on a small table that stood between us. The glasses had been filled. The sherry sparkled.

I stared at the glass nearest me, trying to make out if the liquid in it was cloudier than that in the other glass. But there appeared to be no difference.

I decided I would not take any chances. It was a round tray, made of smooth Kashmiri walnut wood. I turned it round with my index finger, so that the glasses changed places.

'Why did you do that?' asked Uncle Bill.

'It's a custom in these parts. You turn the tray with the sun, a complete revolution. It brings good luck.'

Uncle Bill looked thoughtful for a few moments, then said, 'Well, let's have some more luck,' and turned the tray around again.

'Now you've spoilt it,' I said. 'You're not supposed to keep revolving it! That's bad luck. I'll have to turn it about again to cancel out the bad luck.'

The tray swung round once more, and Uncle Bill had the glass that was meant for me.

'Cheers!' I said, and drank from my glass.

It was good sherry.

Uncle Bill hesitated. Then he shrugged, said 'Cheers', and drained his glass quickly.

But he did not offer to fill the glasses again.

Early next morning he was taken violently ill. I heard him retching in his room, and I got up and went to see if there was anything I could do. He was groaning, his head hanging over the side of the bed. I brought him a basin and a jug of water.

'Would you like me to fetch a doctor?' I asked.

He shook his head. 'No I'll be all right. It must be something I ate.'

'It's probably the water. It's not too good at this time of the year. Many people come down with gastric trouble during their first few days in Fosterganj.'

'Ah, that must be it,' he said, and doubled up as a fresh spasm of pain and nausea swept over him.

He was better by evening—whatever had gone into the glass must have been by way of the preliminary dose and a day later he was well enough to pack his suitcase and announce his departure. The climate of Fosterganj did not agree with him, he told me.

Just before he left, I said; 'Tell me, Uncle, why did you drink it?'

'Drink what? The water?'

'No, the glass of sherry into which you'd slipped one of your famous powders.'

He gaped at me, then gave a nervous whinnying laugh. 'You will have your little joke, won't you?'

'No, I mean it,' I said. 'Why did you drink the stuff? It was meant for me, of course.'

He looked down at his shoes, then gave a little shrug and turned away.

'In the circumstances,' he said, 'it seemed the only decent thing to do.'

I'll say this for Uncle Bill: he was always the perfect gentleman.

Hanging at the Mango-Tope

The two captive policemen, Inspector Hukam Singh and Sub-Inspector Guler Singh, were being pushed unceremoniously along the dusty, deserted, sun-drenched road. The people of the village had made themselves scarce. They would reappear only when the dacoits went away.

The leader of the dacoit gang was Mangal Singh Bundela, great-grandson of a Pindari adventurer who had been a thorn in the side of the British. Mangal was doing his best to be a thorn in the flesh of his own government. The local police force had been strengthened recently, but it was still inadequate for dealing with the dacoits who knew the ravines better than any surveyor. The dacoit Mangal had made a fortune out of ransom: his chief victims were the sons of wealthy industrialists, moneylenders or landowners. But today he had captured two police officials; of no value as far as ransom went, but prestigious prisoners who could be put to other uses....

Mangal Singh wanted to show off in front of the police. He would kill at least one of them—his reputation demanded it—

but he would let the other go, in order that his legendary power and ruthlessness be given a maximum publicity. A legend is always a help!

His red and green turban was tied rakishly to one side. His dhoti extended right down to his ankles. His slippers were embroidered with gold and silver thread. His weapon was no ancient matchlock, but a well-greased 303 rifle. Two of his men had similar rifles. Some had revolvers. Only the smaller fry carried swords or country-made pistols. Mangal Singh's gang, though traditional in many ways, was up-to-date in the matter of weapons. Right now they had the policemen's guns too.

'Come along, Inspector sahib,' said Mangal Singh, in tones of police barbarity, tugging at the rope that encircled the stout Inspector's midriff. 'Had you captured me today, you would have been a hero. You would have taken all the credit, even though you could not keep up with your men in the ravines. Too bad you chose to remain sitting in your jeep with the Sub-Inspector. The jeep will be useful to us, you will not. But I would like you to be a hero all the same—and there is none better than a dead hero!'

Mangal Singh's followers doubled up with laughter. They loved their leader's cruel sense of humour.

'As for you, Guler Singh,' he continued, giving his attention to the Sub-Inspector, 'You are a man from my own village. You should have joined me long ago. But you were never to be trusted. You thought there would be better pickings in the police, didn't you?'

Guler Singh said nothing, simply hung his head and wondered what his fate would be. He felt certain that Mangal Singh would devise some diabolical and fiendish method of dealing with his captives. Guler Singh's only hope was Constable Ghanshyam, who hadn't been caught by the dacoits because, at the time of the ambush, he had been in the bushes relieving himself.

'To the mango-tope!' said Mangal Singh, prodding the policemen forward.

'Listen to me, Mangal,' said the perspiring Inspector, who was ready to try anything to get out of his predicament. 'Let me go, and I give you my word there'll be no trouble for you in this area as long as I am posted here. What could be more convenient than that?'

'Nothing,' said Mangal Singh. 'But your word isn't good. *My* word is different. I have told my men that I will hang you at the mango-tope, and I mean to keep my word. But I believe in fair-play—I like a little sport! You may yet go free if your friend here, Sub-Inspector Guler Singh, has his wits about him.'

The Inspector and his subordinate exchanged doubtful puzzled looks. They were not to remain puzzled for long. On reaching the mango-tope, the dacoits produced a good strong hemp rope, one end looped into a slip-knot. Many a garland of marigolds had the Inspector received during his mediocre career. Now, for the first time, he was being garlanded with a hangman's noose. He had seen hangings; he had rather enjoyed them; but he had no stomach for his own. The Inspector begged for mercy. Who wouldn't have, in his position?

'Be quiet,' commanded Mangal Singh. 'I do not want to know about your wife and your children and the manner in which they will starve. You shot my son last year.'

'Not I!' cried the Inspector. 'It was some other.'

'You led the party. But now, just to show you that I'm a sporting fellow, I am going to have you strung up from this tree, and then I am going to give Guler Singh six shots with a rifle and if he can sever the rope that suspends you before you are dead, well then, you can remain alive and I will let you go! For your sake, I hope the Sub-Inspector's aim is good. He will have to shoot fast. My man Phambiri, who has made this noose, was once executioner in a city jail. He guarantees that you won't last more than fifteen seconds at the end of *his* rope.'

Guler Singh was taken to a spot about forty yards. A rifle was thrust into his hands. Two dacoits clambered into the branches of the mango tree. The Inspector, his hands tied behind, could only gaze at them in horror. His mouth opened and shut as though he already had need of more air. And then, suddenly, the rope went taut, up went the Inspector, his throat caught in a vice, while the branch of the tree shook and mango-blossoms fluttered to the ground. The Inspector dangled from the rope, his feet about three feet about the ground.

'You can shoot,' said Mangal Singh, nodding to the Sub-Inspector.

And Guler Singh, his hands trembling a little, raised the rifle to his shoulder and fired three shots in rapid succession. But the rope was swinging violently and the Inspector's body was jerking about like a fish on a hook. The bullets went wide.

Guler Singh found the magazine empty. He reloaded, wiped the stinging sweat from his eyes, raised the rifle again, took more careful aim. His hands were steadier now. He rested the sights on the upper portion of the rope, where there was less motion. Normally he was a good shot, but he had never been asked to demonstrate his skill in circumstances such as these.

The Inspector still gyrated at the end of his rope. There was life in him yet. His face was purple. The world, in those choking moments, was a medley of upside-down roofs and a red sun spinning slowly towards him.

Guler Singh's rifle cracked again. An inch or two wide this time. But the fifth shot found its mark, sending small tuffs of rope winging into the air.

The shot did not sever the rope; it was only a nick.

Guler Singh had one shot left. He was quite calm. The rifle-sight followed the rope's swing, less agitated now that the Inspector's convulsions were lessening. Guler Singh felt sure he could sever the rope this time.

And then, as his finger touched the trigger, an odd, disturbing thought slipped into his mind, hung there, throbbing: 'Whose life are you trying to save? Hukam Singh has stood in the way of your promotion more than once. He had you charge-sheeted for accepting fifty rupees from an unlicensed rickshaw-puller. He makes you do all the dirty work, blames you when things go wrong, takes the credit when there is credit to be taken. But for him, you'd be an Inspector!'

The rope swayed slightly to the right. The rifle moved just a fraction to the left. The last shot rang out, clipping a sliver of bark from the mango tree.

The Inspector was dead when they cut him down.

'Bad luck,' said Mangal Singh Bundela. 'You nearly saved him. But the next time I catch up with you, Guler Singh, it will be your turn to hang from the mango tree. So keep well away! You know that I am a man of my word. I keep it now, by giving you your freedom.'

A few minutes later the party of dacoits had melted away into the late afternoon shadows of the scrub forest. There was the sound of a jeep starting up. Then silence—a silence so profound that it seemed to be shouting in Guler Singh's ears.

As the village people began to trickle out of their houses, Constable Ghanshyam appeared as if from nowhere, swearing that he had lost his way in the jungle. Several people had seen the incident from their windows; they were unanimous in praising the Sub-Inspector for his brave attempt to save his superior's life. He had done his best.

'It is true,' thought Guler Singh. 'I did my best.'

That moment of hesitation before the last shot, the question that had suddenly reared up in the darkness of his mind, had already gone from his memory. We remember only what we want to remember.

'I did my best,' he told everyone.

And so he had.

Eyes of the Cat

I wrote this little story for the schoolgirl who said my stories weren't scary enough. Her comment was 'Not bad', and she gave me seven out of ten.

Her eyes seemed flecked with gold when the sun was on them. And as the sun set over the mountains, drawing a deep red wound across the sky, there was more than gold in Kiran's eyes. There was anger; for she had been cut to the quick by some remarks her teacher had made—the culmination of weeks of insults and taunts.

Kiran was poorer than most of the girls in her class and could not afford the tuitions that had become almost obligatory if one was to pass and be promoted. 'You'll have to spend another year in the ninth,' said Madam. 'And if you don't like that, you can find another school—a school where it won't matter if your blouse is torn and your tunic is old and your shoes are falling apart.' Madam had shown her large teeth in what was supposed to be a good-natured smile, and all the girls had tittered dutifully. Sycophancy had become part of the curriculum in Madam's private academy for girls.

On the way home in the gathering gloom, Kiran's two companions commiserated with her.

'She's a mean old thing,' said Aarti. 'She doesn't care for anyone but herself.'

'Her laugh reminds me of a donkey braying,' said Sunita, who was more forthright.

But Kiran wasn't really listening. Her eyes were fixed on some point in the far distance, where the pines stood in silhouette against a night sky that was growing brighter every moment. The moon was rising, a full moon, a moon that meant something very special to Kiran, that made her blood tingle and her skin prickle and her hair glow and send out sparks. Her steps seemed to grow lighter, her limbs more sinewy as she moved gracefully, softly over the mountain path.

Abruptly she left her companions at a fork in the road.

'I'm taking the short cut through the forest,' she said.

Her friends were used to her sudden whims. They knew she was not afraid of being alone in the dark. But Kiran's moods made them feel a little nervous, and now, holding hands, they hurried home along the open road.

The short cut took Kiran through the dark oak forest. The crooked, tormented branches of the oaks threw twisted shadows across the path. A jackal howled at the moon; a nightjar called from urgency, and her breath came in short, sharp gasps. Bright moonlight bathed the hillside when she reached her home on the outskirts of the village.

Refusing her dinner, she went straight to her small room and flung the window open. Moonbeams crept over the window-sill and over her arms which were already covered with golden hair. Her strong nails had shredded the rotten wood of the window-sill.

Tail swishing and ears pricked, the tawny leopard came swiftly out of the window, crossed the open field behind the house, and melted into the shadows.

A little later it padded silently through the forest.

Although the moon shone brightly on the tin-roofed town, the leopard knew where the shadows were deepest and merged beautifully with them. An occasional intake of breath, which resulted in a short rasping cough, was the only sound it made.

Madam was returning from dinner at a ladies' club, called the Kitten Club as a sort of foil to the husbands' club affiliations. There were still a few people in the street, and while no one could help noticing Madam, who had the contours of a steam-roller, none saw or heard the predator who had slipped down a side alley and reached the steps of the teacher's house. It sat there silently, waiting with all the patience of an obedient schoolgirl.

When Madam saw the leopard on her steps, she dropped her handbag and opened her mouth to scream; but her voice would not materialise. Nor would her tongue ever be used again, either to savour chicken biryani or to pour scorn upon her pupils, for the leopard had sprung at her throat, broken her neck, and dragged her into the bushes.

In the morning, when Aarti and Sunita set out for school, they stopped as usual at Kiran's cottage and called out to her.

Kiran was sitting in the sun, combing her long black hair.

'Aren't you coming to school today, Kiran?' asked the girls.

'No, I won't bother to go today,' said Kiran. She felt lazy, but pleased with herself, like a contented cat.

'Madam won't be pleased,' said Aarti. 'Shall we tell her you're sick?'

'It won't be necessary,' said Kiran, and gave them one of her mysterious smiles. 'I'm sure it's going to be a holiday.'

A Little Song of Love

The wild rose is blooming
And new leaves shine green,
The sky when it's open
Is ultramarine.

Sleep well, my darling,
Keep dreaming, stay warm,
The blackbird is singing
To tell us it's down.

The wild geese are winging
Their way to the north,
And I know from their calling
It's time we went forth.

The spring sap is rising
As we set out together,
And you'll be my sweetheart
For ever and ever.

Binya Passes By

The author looks back on a love of long ago. 'It isn't time that's passing by; it is you and I...'

While I was walking home one day, along the path through the pines, I heard a girl singing.

It was summer in the hills, and the trees were in new leaf. The walnuts and cherries were just beginning to form between the leaves.

The wind was still and the trees were hushed, and the song came to me clearly; but it was not the words—which I could not follow—or the rise and fall of the melody which held me in thrall, but the voice itself, which was a young and tender voice.

I left the path and scrambled down the slope, slipping on fallen pine needles. But when I came to the bottom of the slope, the singing had stopped and no one was there. 'I'm sure I heard someone singing,' I said to myself; but I may have been wrong. In the hills it is always possible to be wrong.

So I walked on home, and presently I heard another song, but this time it was the whistling thrush rendering a broken melody, singing of dark, sweet secrets in the depths of the forest.

I had little to sing about myself, as the electricity bill hadn't been paid, and there was nothing in the bank, and my second novel had just been turned down by another publisher. Still, it was summer, and men and animals were drowsy, and so too were my creditors. The distant mountains loomed purple in the shimmering dust-haze.

I walked through the pines again, but I did not hear the singing. And then for a week I did not leave the cottage, as the novel had to be rewritten, and I worked hard at it, pausing only to eat and sleep and take note of the leaves turning a darker green.

The window opened on to the forest. Trees reached up to the window. Oak, maple, walnut. Higher up the hill, the pines started, and further on, armies of deodars marched over the mountains. And the mountains rose higher, and the trees grew stunted until they finally disappeared and only the black spirit-haunted rocks rose up to meet the everlasting snows. Those peaks cradled the sky. I could not see them from my windows. But on clear mornings they could be seen from the pass on the Tehri road.

There was a stream at the bottom of the hill. One morning, quite early, I went down to the stream, and using the boulders as stepping-stones, moved downstream for about half a mile. Then I lay down to rest on a flat rock, in the shade of a wild cherry tree, and watched the sun shifting through the branches as it rose over the hill called Pari Tibba (Fairy Hill) and slid down the steep slope into the valley. The air was very still and already the birds were silent. The only sound came from the water running over the stony bed of the stream. I had lain there ten, perhaps fifteen, minutes when I began to feel that someone was watching me.

Someone in the trees, in the shadows, still and watchful. Nothing moved; not a stone shifted, not a twig broke; but someone was watching me. I felt terribly exposed; not to danger, but to the scrutiny of unknown eyes. So I left the rock and, finding a path through the trees, began climbing the hill again.

It was warm work. The sun was up, and there was no breeze. I was perspiring profusely by the time I got to the top of the hill. There was no sign of my unseen watcher. Two lean cows grazed on the short grass; the tinkling of their bells was the only sound in the sultry summer air.

That song again! The same song, the same singer. I heard her from my window. And putting aside the book I was reading, I leant out of the window and started down through the trees. But the foliage was too heavy, and the singer too far away for me to be able to make her out. 'Should I go and look for her?' I wondered. Or is it better this way—heard but not seen? For having fallen in love with a song, must it follow that I will fall in love with the singer? No. But surely it is the voice, and not the song that has touched me... Presently the singing ended, and I turned away from the window.

A girl was gathering bilberries on the hillside. She was fresh-faced, honey-coloured; her lips were stained with purple juice. She smiled at me. 'Are they good to eat?' I asked.

She opened her fist and thrust out her hand, which was full of berries, bruised and crushed. I took one and put it in my mouth. It had a sharp, sour taste. 'It is good,' I said. Finding that I could speak haltingly in her language, she came nearer, said, 'Take more then,' and filled my hand with bilberries. Her fingers touched mine. The sensation was almost unique; for it was nine or ten years since my hand had touched a girl's.

'Where do you live?' I asked. She pointed across the valley to where a small village straddled the slopes of a terraced hill.

'It's quite far,' I said. 'Do you always come so far from home?'

'I go further than this,' she said. 'The cows must find fresh grass. And there is wood to gather and grass to cut.' She showed me the sickle held by the cloth tied firmly about her waist. 'Sometimes I go to the top of Pari Tibba, sometimes to the valley beyond. Have you been there?'

'No. But I will go some day.'

'It is always windy on Pari Tibba.'

'Is it true that there are fairies there?'

She laughed. 'That is what people say. But those are people who have never been there. I do not see fairies on Pari Tibba. It is said that there are ghosts in the ruins on the hill. But I do not see any ghosts.'

'I have heard of the ghosts,' I said. 'Two lovers who ran away and took shelter in a ruined cottage. At night there was a storm, and they were killed by lightning. Is it true, this story?'

'It happened many years ago, before I was born. I have heard the story. But there are no ghosts on Pari Tibba.'

'How old are you?' I asked.

'Fifteen, sixteen, I do not know for sure.'

'Doesn't your mother know?'

'She is dead. And my grandmother has forgotten. And my brother, he is younger than me and he's forgotten his own age. Is it important to remember?'

'No, it is not important. Not here, anyway. Not in the hills. To a mountain, a hundred years are but as a day.'

'Are you very old?' she asked.

'I hope not. Do I look very old?'

'Only a hundred,' she said, and laughed, and the silver bangles on her wrists tinkled as she put her hand up to her laughing face.

'Why do you laugh?' I asked.

'Because you looked as though you believed me. How old are you?'

'Thirty-five, thirty-six, I do not remember.'

'Ah, it is better to forget!'

'That's true,' I said, 'but sometimes one has to fill in forms and things like that, and then one has to state one's age.'

'I have never filled a form. I have never seen one.'

'And I hope you never will. It is a piece of paper covered with useless information. It is all a part of human progress.'

'Progress?'

'Yes. Are you unhappy?'

'No.'

'Do you go hungry?'

'No.'

'Then you don't need progress. Wild bilberries are better.'

She went away without saying goodbye. The cows had strayed and she ran after them, calling them by name: 'Neelu, Neelu!' (Blue) and 'Bhuri!' (Old One). Her bare feet moved swiftly over the rocks and dry grass.

Early May. The cicadas were singing in the forests; or rather, orchestrating, since they make the sound with their legs. The whistling thrushes pursued each other over the tree-tops, in acrobatic love-flights. Sometimes the langurs visited the oak trees, to feed on the leaves. As I moved down the path to the stream, I heard the same singing; and coming suddenly upon the clearing near the water's edge, I saw the girl sitting on a rock, her feet in the rushing water—the same girl who had given me bilberries. Strangely enough, I had not guessed that she was the singer. Unseen voices conjure up fanciful images. I had imagined a woodland nymph, a graceful, delicate, beautiful, goddess-like creature; not a mischievous-eyed, round-faced, juice-stained, slightly ragged pixie. Her dhoti—a rough, homespun sari—faded and torn; an impractical garment, I thought, for running about on the hillside, but the village folk put their girls into dhotis before they are twelve. She'd compromised by hitching it up, and by strengthening the waist with a length of cloth bound tightly about her, but she'd have been more at ease in the long, flounced skirt worn in the further hills.

But I was not disillusioned. I had clearly taken a fancy to her cherubic, open countenance; and the sweetness of her voice added to her charms.

I watched her from the banks of the stream, and presently she looked up, grinned, and stuck her tongue out at me.

'That's a nice way to greet me,' I said. 'Have I offended you?'

'You surprised me. Why did you not call out?'

'Because I was listening to your singing. I did not wish to speak until you had finished.'

'It was only a song.'

'But you sang it sweetly.'

She smiled. 'Have you brought anything to eat?'

'No. Are you hungry?'

'At this time I get hungry. When you come to meet me you must always bring something to eat.'

'But I didn't come to meet you. I didn't know you would be here.'

'You do not wish to meet me?'

'I didn't mean that. It is nice to meet you.'

'You will meet me if you keep coming into the forest. So always bring something to eat.'

'I will do so next time. Shall I pick you some berries?'

'You will have to go to the top of the hill again to find the kingora bushes.'

'I don't mind. If you are hungry, I will bring some.'

'All right,' she said, and looked down at her feet, which were still in the water.

Like some knight-errant of old, I toiled up the hill again until I found the bilberry bushes; and stuffing my pockets with berries, I returned to the stream. But when I got there I found she'd slipped away. The cowbells tinkled on the far hill.

Glow-worms shone fitfully in the dark. The night was full of sounds—the tonk-tonk of a nightjar, the cry of a barking deer, the shuffling of porcupines, the soft flip-flop of moths beating against the windowpanes. On the hill across the valley, lights flickered in the small village—the dim lights of kerosene lamps swinging in the dark.

'What is your name?' I asked, when we met again on the path through the pine forest.

'Binya,' she said. 'What is yours?'

'I've no name.'

'All right, Mr No-name.'

'I mean, I haven't made a name for myself. We must make our own names, don't you think?'

'Binya is my name. I do not wish to have any other. Where are you going?'

'Nowhere.'

'No-name goes nowhere! Then you cannot come with me, because I am going home and my grandmother will set the village dogs on you if you follow me.' And laughing, she ran down the path to the stream; she knew I could not catch up with her.

Her face streamed summer rain as she climbed the steep hill, calling the white cow home. She seemed very tiny on the windswept mountainside; a twist of hair lay flat against her forehead, and her torn blue dhoti clung to her firm round thighs. I went to her with an umbrella to give her shelter. She stood with me beneath the umbrella and let me put my arm around her. Then she turned her face up to mine, wonderingly, and I kissed her quickly, softly on the lips. Her lips tasted of raindrops and mint. And then she left me there, so gallant in the blistering rain. She ran home laughing. But it was worth the drenching.

Another day I heard her calling to me—'No-name, Mister No-name!'—but I couldn't see her, and it was some time before I found her, halfway up a cherry tree, her feet pressed firmly against the bark, her dhoti tucked up between her thighs—fai rounded thighs, and legs that were strong and vigorous.

'The cherries are not ripe,' I said.

'They are never ripe. But I like them green and sour. Will you come into the tree?'

'If I can still climb a tree,' I said.

'My grandmother is over sixty, and *she* can climb trees.'

'Well, I wouldn't mind being more adventurous at sixty. There's not so much to lose then.' I climbed into the tree without much difficulty, but I did not think the higher branches would take my weight; so I remained standing in the fork of the tree, my face on a level with Binya's breasts. I put my hand against her waist, and kissed her on the soft inside of her arm. She did not say anything. But she took me by the hand and helped me to climb a little higher, and I put my arm around her, as much to support myself as to be close to her.

The full moon rides high, shining through the tall oak trees near the window. The night is full of sounds, crickets, the tonk-tonk of a nightjar, and floating across the valley from your village, the sound of drums beating, and people singing. It is a festival day, and there will be feasting in your home. Are you singing too, tonight? And are you thinking of me, as you sing, as you laugh, as you dance with your friends? I am sitting here alone, and so I have no one to think of but you.

Binya...I take your name again and again—as though by taking it, I can make you hear me, come to me, walking over the moonlit mountain....

are spirits abroad tonight. They move silently in the ey hover about the window at which I sit; they take the wind and rush about the house. Spirits of the trees, its of the old house. An old lady died here last year. She'd lived in the house for over thirty years; something of her personality surely dwells here still. When I look into the tall, old mirror which was hers, I sometimes catch a glimpse of her pale face and long, golden hair. She likes me, I think, and the house is kind to me. Would she be jealous of you, Binya?

The music and singing grows louder. I can imagine your face glowing in the firelight. Your eyes shine with laughter. You have all those people near you and I have only the stars, and the nightjar, and the ghost in the mirror.

I woke early, while the dew was still fresh on the grass, and walked down the hill to the stream, and then up to a little knoll where a pine tree grew in solitary splendour, the wind going *hoo-hoo* in its slender branches. This was my favourite place, my place of power, where I came to renew myself from time to time. I lay on the grass, dreaming. The sky in its blueness swung round above me. An eagle soared in the distance. I heard her voice down among the trees; or I thought I heard it. But when I went to look, I could not find her.

I'd always prided myself on my rationality; had taught myself to be wary of emotional states, like 'falling in love', which turned out to be ephemeral and illusory. And although I told myself again and again that the attraction was purely physical, on my part as well as hers, I had to admit to myself that my feelings towards Binya differed from the feelings I'd had for others; and that while sex had often been for me a celebration, it had, like any other feast, resulted in satiety, a need for change, a desire to forget....

Binya represented something else—something wild, dream-like, fairy-like. She moved close to the spirit-haunted rocks, the old trees, the young grass; she had absorbed something from them—a primeval innocence, an unconcern with the passing of time and events, an affinity with the forest and the mountains; this made her special and magical.

And so, when three, four, five days went by, and I did not find her on the hillside, I went through all the pangs of frustrated love: had she forgotten me and gone elsewhere? Had we been seen together, and was she being kept at home? Was she ill? Or, had she been spirited away?

I could hardly go and ask for her. I would probably be driven from the village. It straddled the opposite hill, a cluster of slate-roof houses, a pattern of little terraced fields. I could see figures in the fields, but they were too far away, too tiny for me to be able to recognise anyone. She had gone to her mother's village a hundred miles away, or so a small boy told me.

And so I brooded; walked disconsolately through the oak forest hardly listening to the birds—the sweet-throated whistling thrush; the shrill barbet; the mellow-voiced doves. Happiness had always made me more responsive to nature. Feeling miserable, my thoughts turned inward. I brooded upon the trickery of time and circumstance; I felt the years were passing by, *had* passed by, like waves on a receding tide, leaving me washed up like a bit of flotsam on a lonely beach. But at the same time, the thrush seemed to mock at me, calling tantalisingly shadows of the ravine; 'It isn't time that's passing by, and I, it is you and I....'

Then I forced myself to snap out of my melancholy. I kept away from the hillside and the forest. I did not look towards the village. I buried myself in my work, tried to think objectively, and wrote an article on 'The inscriptions on the iron pillar at Kalsi'; very learned, very dry, very sensible.

But at night I was assailed by the thoughts of Binya. I could not sleep. I switched on the light, and there she was, smiling at me from the looking glass, replacing the image of the old lady who had watched over me for so long.

Love and Cricket

It was a quiet day in New Delhi. Everyone was indoors, watching an India-Pakistan cricket match on TV. Even the hotel seemed understaffed. I'd given up on cricket years ago, after a long and uninteresting career as twelfth man for the Chutmalpur Club team. Carrying out the drinks or fielding in the hot sun on behalf of others had finally soured my attitude towards the game. Now my greatest pleasure was sitting in a shady spot, sipping a cool drink brought to me by an agile young waiter, who would no doubt have preferred to be out on a cricket field.

It was an elderly waiter who brought me the nimbu-pani. The younger ones were probably crowded around a TV set in the kitchen. I relaxed in the easy chair of the hotel's garden restaurant, here I was an occasional customer. Sweet-peas filled the air with their heady perfume. Snapdragons snapped in the mid-March sunshine. A carpet of soft pink phlox was soothing to the eyes. New Delhi in the spring is kind to flower gardens.

I had the place to myself. I felt at peace with the world. The garden was quiet and restful—until two noisy children, must have been about twelve, and a girl a little came charging out of the shadows, kicking a rubber nd. Having played football myself once, I looked at game with amused tolerance; that is, until the boy, bending it like Beckham, sent the ball crashing on to my table, upsetting my nimbu-pani.

The elderly waiter came running to my rescue. The children fled, concealing themselves behind some potted palms. Their mother appeared on the steps, threatening them with dire consequences. She walked over to me, apologising.

'I'm so sorry. They are very naughty.'

'That's all right,' I said, 'Just high spirits. And it seems to be the season for ball games.'

The sun was in my eyes and I couldn't see her very well. She was about forty, on the plump side, dark and quite attractive.

'It's perfectly all right,' I said again, as the waiter brought me another nimbu-pani.

She just stood there, staring at me

'Weren't you—aren't you—Rusty?'

I looked at her more closely then. It was a long time since anyone had called me Rusty. I stood up so that the sun wouldn't be in my eyes. There was something about *her* eyes, soft and gentle, and her hair, still lustrous, and her lips of course, that reminded me of——

'Sushila?' I said hesitantly. Could it really be her—grown chubby and middle-aged and maternal? Sushila, my lost love of twenty plus years ago....

'Yes, I am Sushila. And you are Rusty. A little older now.'

'And grown quite rusty over the years.' I took her hand and

asked her to join me. 'And call the children over.' But the children had made themselves scarce.

'They must have gone to play video games.' She sat down without any hesitation. 'It will be nice to talk to you. It's so boring staying in these big hotels.'

I called the waiter over and she ordered an orange drink. I raised my glass and looked at her through the translucent liquid. She had worn well with the years—much better than I had! Although youth had flown, vestiges of youthfulness remained in her dimpled smile, full lips and lively glance. Her once slim hand was now a chubby hand; but all the same, it would be nice to touch it, and I did so, allowing my fingers to rest lightly against her palm. She drew her hand away, but not too quickly.

'So, now you're a mother of two,' I remarked, by way of making conversation.

'Three,' she said. 'My eldest boy is at boarding. He's fifteen. You never married?'

'Not after you turned me down.'

'I did not turn you down. It was my parents' wish.'

'I know. It wasn't your fault—and it wasn't theirs. I had no money, and no prospects. It wouldn't have been fair to you. And I would have had to give up my writing and take some miserable job.'

'Would you have done that for me?'

'Of course, I loved you.'

'But now you are successful. Had you married me, you would not be so well-known.'

'Who knows? I might have done better. Your husband must be very successful to be staying here.'

'Ah, but he's in business. In Bombay, a stockbroker. I know nothing about it. I'm just a housewife.'

'Well, three children must keep you pretty busy.'

We were silent for some time. Traffic hummed along nearby Janpath, but it was quiet in the garden. You could even hear the cooing of doves from the verandah roof. A hoopoe hopped across the grass, looking for insects.

Twenty years ago we had held hands and walked barefoot across the grass on the little hillock overlooking the stream that tumbled down to Mossy Falls. I still have photographs taken that day. Her cousin had gone paddling downstream, looking for coloured pebbles, and I had taken advantage of his absence by kissing her, first on the cheeks, and then, quite suddenly, on the lips.

Now she seemed to be recalling the same incident because she said, 'You were very romantic, Rusty.'

'I'm still romantic. But the modern world has no time for romance. It's all done on computers now. Make love by e-mail. It's much safer.'

'And you preferred the moonlight.'

'Ah, those full moon nights, do you remember them? The moon coming up over the top of Landour, and then pouring through the windows of Maplewood.... And you put your head against my shoulder and I held you there until a cloud came across the moon. And then you let me kiss you everywhere.'

'I don't remember that.'

'Of course you do.'

'What happened to your bicycle? The one you used to sing about.'

'The bicycle went the way of all machines. There were others. But the song still lingers on. My grandfather used to sing it to my grandmother, before they were married. There it is—.' And I sang it again, sofly, with the old waiter listening intently in the background:

'Daisy, Daisy, give me your answer, do!
I'm half crazy all for the love of you!
It won't be a stylish marriage,
As I can't afford a carriage,
But you'll look sweet upon the seat
Of a bicycle built for two.'

Sushila laughed and clapped her hands. The waiter smiled and nodded his approval.

'And your grandparents—were they happy with a bicycle?'

'Very happy. That's all they had for years. But I see you have a new BMW. Very nice.'

The children were waving to her from a parked car. 'We have to go shopping,' she said. 'But not until the match is over.'

'Well, it's only lunch time. The game will finish at five.'

Something buzzed in her handbag, and she opened it and took out a mobile. Yes, my dear old Sushila, simple sweetheart of my youth, was now equipped with the latest technology. She listened carefully to what someone was saying, then switched off with a look of resignation.

'No shopping?' I asked.

'No shopping. He bet on Tendulkar making a duck.'

'And what did he score?'

'A hundred. My husband lost a lakh. It's nothing. Would you like to have lunch with us? It's so boring here.'

'No,' I said.' I have to go.'

'Back to your lonely cottage in the hills?'

'Yes, eventually. I come here sometimes, when I'm in Delhi. I like the flower garden. But I'm staying with friends.' As I got up to go, she gave me her hand.

'Will you come again?'

'I can't say. But it was great meeting you, Sushila. You look lovelier than ever. Even when you're bored.'

I gave the waiter a generous tip, and he followed me out to the parking lot and very respectfully dusted off the seat of my bicycle. I wobbled down the road to Janpath, humming the tune of that well-remembered song.

We Must Love Someone

We must love someone
If we are to justify
Our presence on this earth.
We must keep loving all our days,
Someone, anyone, anywhere
Outside ourselves;
For even the sarus crane
Will grieve over its lost companion,
And the seal its mate.
Somewhere in life
There must be someone
To take your hand
And share the torrid day.
Without the touch of love
There is no life, and we must fade away.

At the Grave of John Mildenhall in Agra

In the year 1594,
Visiting first Lahore
And then the garden city of Ajmer,
Came a merchant adventurer,
John Mildenhall by name,
From London by the River Thame.
To Agra's mart he brought
His goods and baggage; then sought
Audience with the great
Moghul, who sat in state
In vast red sandstone audience-hall.
'We are pleased, Mr Mildenhall,
To have you at our court,' great Akbar said;
'Your Queen is known to have an astute head,
Your country many ships, and I hear
Of a poet called Shakespeare—

Who, though not as good as Fazl or Faiz,
Writes a pretty line and does plays on the side.
But tell us—when will you be on your way?'

'Most gracious King, I'd like to stay—
With your permission—for a while,'
Said the traveller with the Elizabethan smile.

To this request the Emperor complied.
John stayed, and settled down, and died.
Over three hundred years had passed
When those who followed, left at last.

Grandpa Fights an Ostrich

Before my grandfather joined the Indian Railways, he worked for a few years on the East African Railways, and it was during that period that he had his now famous encounter with the ostrich. My childhood was frequently enlivened by this oft-told tale of his, and I give it here in his own words—or as well as I can remember them!

While engaged in the laying of a new railway line, I had a miraculous escape from an awful death. I lived in a small township, but my work lay some twelve miles away, and I had to go to the work-site and back on horseback.

One day, my horse had a slight accident, so I decided to do the journey on foot, being a great walker in those days. I also knew of a short cut through the hills that would save me about six miles.

This short cut went through an ostrich farm—or 'camp', as it was called. It was the breeding season. I was fairly familiar with the ways of ostriches, and knew that male birds were very aggressive in the breeding season, ready to attack on the slightest provocation, but I also knew that my dog would scare away any bird that might try to attack me. Strange though it may seem, even the biggest ostrich (and some of them grow to a height of nine feet) will run faster than a racehorse at the sight of even a small dog. So, I felt quite safe in the company of my dog, a mongrel who had adopted me some two months previously.

On arrival at the 'camp', I climbed through the wire fencing and, keeping a good look-out, dodged across the open spaces between the thorn bushes. Now and then I caught a glimpse of the birds feeding some distance away.

I had gone about half a mile from the fencing when up started a hare. In an instant my dog gave chase. I tried calling him back, even though I knew it was hopeless. Chasing hares was that dog's passion.

I don't know whether it was the dog's bark or my own shouting, but what I was most anxious to avoid immediately happened. The ostriches were startled and began darting to and fro. Suddenly, I saw a big male bird emerge from a thicket about a hundred yards away. He stood still and stared at me for a few moments. I stared back. Then, expanding his short wings and with his tail erect, he came bounding towards me.

As I had nothing, not even a stick, with which to defend myself, I turned and ran towards the fence. But it was an unequal race. What were my steps of two or three feet against the creature's great strides of sixteen to twenty feet? There was only one hope: to get behind a large bush and try to elude the bird until help came. A dodging game was my only chance.

And so, I rushed for the nearest clump of thorn bushes and waited for my pursuer. The great bird wasted no time—he was immediately upon me.

Then the strangest encounter took place. I dodged this way and that, taking great care not to get directly in front of the ostrich's deadly kick. Ostriches kick forward, and with such terrific force that if you were struck, their huge chisel-like nails would cause you much damage.

I was breathless, and really quite helpless, calling wildly for help as I circled the thorn bush. My strength was ebbing. How much longer could I keep going? I was ready to drop from exhaustion.

As if aware of my condition, the infuriated bird suddenly doubled back on his course and charged straight at me. With a desperate effort I managed to step to one side. I don't know how, but I found myself holding on to one of the creature's wings, quite close to its body.

It was now the ostrich's turn to be frightened. He began to turn, or rather waltz, moving round and round so quickly that my feet were soon swinging out from his body, almost horizontally! All the while the ostrich kept opening and shutting his beak with loud snaps.

Imagine my situation as I clung desperately to the wing of the enraged bird. He was whirling me round and round as though he were a discus-thrower—and I the discus! My arms soon began to ache with the strain, and the swift and continuous circling was making me dizzy. But I knew that if I relaxed my hold, even for a second, a terrible fate awaited me.

Round and round we went in a great circle. It seemed as if that spiteful bird would never tire. And, I knew I could not hold on much longer. Suddenly the ostrich went into reverse! This unexpected move made me lose my hold and sent me sprawling to the ground. I landed in a heap near the thorn bush and in an instant, before I even had time to realise what had happened, the big bird was upon me. I thought the end had come. Instinctively I raised my hands to protect my face. But the ostrich did not strike.

I moved my hands from my face and there stood the creature with one foot raised, ready to deliver a deadly kick! I couldn't move. Was the bird going to play cat-and-mouse with me, and prolong the agony?

As I watched, frightened and fascinated, the ostrich turned his head sharply to the left. A second later he jumped back, turned, and made off as fast as he could go. Dazed, I wondered what had happened to make him beat so unexpected a retreat.

I soon found out. To my great joy, I heard the bark of my truant dog, and the next moment he was jumping around me, licking my face and hands. Needless to say, I returned his caresses most affectionately! And, I took good care to see that he did not leave my side until we were well clear of that ostrich 'camp'.

The Zigzag Walk

Uncle Ken always maintained that the best way to succeed in life was to zigzag. 'If you keep going off in new directions,' he declared, 'you will meet new career opportunities!'

Well, opportunities certainly came Uncle Ken's way, but he was not a success in the sense that Dale Carnegie or Deepak Chopra would have defined a successful man…

In a long life devoted to 'muddling through' with the help of the family, Uncle Ken's many projects had included a chicken farm (rather like the one operated by Ukridge in Wodehouse's *Love Among the Chickens*) and a mineral water bottling project. For this latter enterprise, he bought a thousand old soda-water bottles and filled them with sulphur water from the springs, five miles from Dehra. It was good stuff, taken in small quantities, but drunk one bottle at a time it proved corrosive—'sulphur and brimstone' as one irate customer described it—and angry buyers demonstrated in front of the house, throwing empty bottles over the wall into grandmother's garden.

Grandmother was furious—more with Uncle Ken than with the demonstrators—and made him give everyone's money back.

'You have to be healthy and strong to take sulphur water,' he explained later.

'I thought it was supposed to make you healthy and strong,' I said.

Grandfather remarked that it did not compare with plain soda-water, which he took with his whisky. 'Why don't you just bottle soda-water?' he said, 'there's a much bigger demand for it.'

But Uncle Ken believed that he had to be original in all things.

'The secret to success is to zigzag,' he said.

'You certainly zigzagged round the garden when your customers were throwing their bottles back at you,' said Grandmother.

Uncle Ken also invented the zigzag walk.

The only way you could really come to know a place well, was to walk in a truly haphazard way. To make a zigzag walk you take the first turning to the left, the first to the right, then the first to the left and so on. It can be quite fascinating provided you are in no hurry to reach your destination. The trouble was that Uncle Ken used this zigzag method even when he had a train to catch.

When Grandmother asked him to go to the station to meet Aunt Mabel and her children, who were arriving from Lucknow, he zigzagged through the town, taking in the botanical gardens in the west and the limestone factories to the east, finally reaching the station by way of the goods yard, in order as he said, 'to take it by surprise'.

Nobody was surprised, least of all Aunt Mabel who had taken a tonga and reached the house while Uncle Ken was still sitting on the station platform, waiting for the next train to come in. I was sent to fetch him.

'Let's zigzag home again,' he said.

'Only on one condition, we eat chaat every fifteen minutes,' I said.

So we went home by way of all the most winding bazaars, and in north-Indian towns they do tend to zigzag, stopping at numerous chaat and halwai shops, until Uncle Ken had finished his money. We got home very late and were scolded by everyone; but as Uncle Ken told me, we were pioneers and had to expect to be misunderstood and even maligned. Posterity would recognise the true value of zigzagging.

'The zigzag way,' he said, 'is the diagonal between heart and reason.'

In our more troubled times, had he taken to preaching on the subject, he might have acquired a large following of dropouts. But Uncle Ken was the original dropout. He would not have tolerated others.

Had he been a space traveller, he would have gone from star to star, zigzagging across the Milky Way.

Uncle Ken would not have succeeded in getting anywhere very fast, but I think he did succeed in getting at least one convert (myself) to see his point: 'When you zigzag, you are not choosing what to see in this world but you are giving the world a chance to see you!'

At Sea with Uncle Ken

With Uncle Ken you had always to expect the unexpected. Even in the most normal circumstances, something unusual would happen to him and to those around him. He was a catalyst for confusion.

My mother should have known better than to ask him to accompany me to England, the year after I'd finished school. She felt that a boy of sixteen was a little too young to make the voyage on his own; I might get lost or lose my money or fall overboard or catch some dreadful disease. She should have realised that Uncle Ken, her only brother (well spoilt by his five sisters), was more likely to do all these things.

Anyway, he was put in charge of me and instructed to deliver me safely to my aunt in England, after which he could either stay there or return to India, whichever he preferred. Granny had paid for his ticket; so in effect he was getting a free holiday which included a voyage on a posh P&O liner.

Our train journey to Bombay passed off without incident, although Uncle Ken did manage to misplace his spectacles, getting down at the station wearing someone else's. This left him a little short-sighted, which might have accounted for his mistaking the stationmaster for a porter and instructing him to look after our luggage.

We had two days in Bombay before boarding the *S.S Strathnaver* and Uncle Ken vowed that we would enjoy ourselves. However, he was a little constrained by his budget and took me to a rather seedy hotel on Lamington Road, where we had to share a toilet with over twenty other people.

'Never mind,' he said. 'We won't spend much time in this dump.' So he took me to Marine Drive and the Gateway of India and to an Irani restaurant in Colaba, where we enjoyed a super dinner of curried prawns and scented rice. I don't know if it was the curry, the prawns, or the scent but Uncle Ken was up all night, running back and forth to that toilet, so that no one else had a chance to use it. Several dispirited travellers simply opened their windows and ejected into space, cursing Uncle Ken all the while.

He had recovered by morning and proposed a trip to the Elephanta Caves. After a breakfast of fish pickle, Malabar chilli chutney and sweet Gujarati puris, we got into a launch, accompanied by several other tourists and set off on our short cruise. The sea was rather choppy and we hadn't gone far before Uncle Ken decided to share his breakfast with the fishes of the sea. He was as green as a seaweed by the time we went ashore. Uncle Ken collapsed on the sand and refused to move, so we didn't see much of the caves. I brought him some coconut water and he revived a bit and suggested we go on a fast until it was time to board our ship.

We were safely on board the following morning, and the ship sailed majestically out from Ballard Pier, Bombay, and India receded into the distance, quite possibly forever as I wasn't sure that I would ever return. The sea fascinated me and I remained on deck all day, gazing at small crafts, passing steamers, sea-birds, the distant shore-line, salt-water smells, the surge of the waves and of course my fellow passengers. I could well understand the fascination it held for writers such as Conrad, Stevenson, Maugham and others.

Uncle Ken, however, remained confined to his cabin. The rolling of the ship made him feel extremely ill. If he had been looking green in Bombay, he was looking yellow at sea. I took my meals in the dining saloon, where I struck up an acquaintance with a well-known palmist and fortune-teller who was on his way to London to make his fortune. He looked at my hand and told me I'd never be rich, but that I'd help other people get rich!

When Uncle Ken felt better (on the third day of the voyage), he struggled up on the deck, took a large lungful of sea air and subsided into a deck-chair. He dozed the day away, but was suddenly wide awake when an attractive blonde strode past us on her way to the lounge. After some time we heard the tinkling of a piano. Intrigued, Uncle Ken rose and staggered into the lounge. The girl was at the piano, playing something classical which wasn't something that Uncle Ken normally enjoyed, but he was smitten by the girl's good looks and stood enraptured, his eyes brightly gleaming, his jaw sagging. With his nose pressed against the glass of the lounge door, he reminded me of a goldfish who had fallen in love with an angel fish that had just been introduced into the tank.

'What is she playing?' he whispered, aware that I had grown up on my father's classical record collection.

'Rachmaninoff,' I made a guess, 'Or maybe Rimsky Korsakov.'

'Something easier to pronounce,' he begged.

'Chopin,' I said.

'And what's his most famous composition?'

'*Polonaise in E flat.* Or may be it's E minor.'

He pushed open the lounge door, walked in, and when the girl had finished playing, applauded loudly. She acknowledged his applause with a smile and then went on to play something else. When she had finished he clapped again and said, 'Wonderful! Chopin never sounded better!'

'Actually, it's Tchaikovsky,' said the girl. But she didn't seem to mind.

Uncle Ken would turn up at all her practice sessions and very soon they were strolling the decks together. She was Australian, on her way to London to pursue a musical career as a concert pianist. I don't know what she saw in Uncle Ken, but he knew all the right people. And he was quite good-looking in an effete sort of way.

Left to my own devices, I followed my fortune-telling friend around and watched him study the palms of our fellow passengers. He foretold romance, travel, success, happiness, health, wealth, and longevity, but never predicted anything that might upset anyone. As he did not charge anything (he was, after all, on holiday) he proved to be a popular passenger throughout the voyage. Later he was to become quite famous as a palmist and mind-reader, an Indian 'Cheiro', much in demand in the capitals of Europe.

The voyage lasted eighteen days, with stops for passengers and cargo at Aden, Port Said, and Marseilles, in that order. It was at Port Said that Uncle Ken and his friend went ashore, to look at the sights and do some shopping.

'You stay on the ship,' Uncle Ken told me. 'Port Said isn't safe for young boys.'

He wanted the girl all to himself, of course. He couldn't have shown off with me around. His 'man of the world' manner would not have been very convincing in my presence.

The ship was due to sail again that evening and passengers had to be back on board an hour before departure. The hours passed easily enough for me as the little library kept me engrossed. If there are books around, I am never bored. Towards evening I went up on deck and saw Uncle Ken's friend coming up the gangway; but of Uncle Ken there was no sign.

'Where's Uncle?' I asked her.

'Hasn't he returned? We got separated in a busy marketplace and I thought he'd get here before me.'

We stood at the railings and looked up and down the pier, expecting to see Uncle Ken among the other returning passengers. But he did not turn up.

'I suppose he's looking for you,' I said. 'He'll miss the boat if he doesn't hurry.'

The ship's hooter sounded. 'All aboard!' called the captain on his megaphone. The big ship moved slowly out of the harbour. We were on our way! In the distance I saw a figure that looked like Uncle Ken running along the pier, frantically waving his arms. But there was no turning back.

A few days later my aunt met me at Tilbury Dock.

'Where's your Uncle Ken?' she asked.

'He stayed behind at Port Said. He went ashore and didn't get back in time.'

'Just like Ken. And I don't suppose he has much money with him. Well, if he gets in touch we'll send him a postal order.'

But Uncle Ken failed to get in touch. He was a topic of discussion for several days, while I settled down in my aunt's house and looked for a job. At sixteen I was working in an office, earning a modest salary and contributing towards my aunt's housekeeping expenses. There was no time to worry about Uncle Ken's whereabouts.

My readers know that I longed to return to India, but it was nearly four years before that became possible. Finally I did come home and as the train drew into Dehra's little station, I looked out of the window and saw a familiar figure on the platform. It was Uncle Ken!

He made no reference to his disappearance at Port Said, and greeted me as though we had last seen each other the previous day.

'I've hired a cycle for you,' he said. 'Feel like a ride?'

'Let me get home first, Uncle Ken. I've got all this luggage.'

The luggage was piled into a tonga, I sat on top of everything and we went clip-clopping down an avenue of familiar lichi trees (all gone now, I fear). Uncle Ken rode behind the tonga, whistling cheerfully.

'When did you get back to Dehra?' I asked.

'Oh, a couple of years ago. Sorry I missed the boat. Was the girl upset?'

'She said she'd never forgive you.'

'Oh well, I expect she's better off without me. Fine piano player. Chopin and all that stuff.'

'Did Granny send you the money to come home?'

'No, I had to take a job working as a waiter in a Greek restaurant. Then I took tourists to look at the pyramids. I'm an expert on pyramids now. Great place, Egypt. But I had to leave when they found I had no papers or permit. They put me on a boat to Aden. Stayed in Aden six months teaching English to the son of a Shiekh. Shiekh's son went to England, I came back to India.'

'And what are you doing now, Uncle Ken?'

'Thinking of starting a poultry farm. Lots of space behind your Gran's house. Maybe you can help with it.'

'I couldn't save much money, Uncle.'

'We'll start in a small way. There is a big demand for eggs, you know. Everyone's into eggs—scrambled, fried, poached, boiled. Egg curry for lunch. Omelettes for dinner. Egg sandwiches for tea. How do you like your egg?'

'Fried,' I said. 'Sunny side up.'

'We shall have fried eggs for breakfast. Funny side up!'

The poultry farm never did happen, but it was good to be back in Dehra, with the prospect of limitless bicycle rides with Uncle Ken.

My Failed Omelettes —and Other Disasters

In nearly fifty years of writing for a living, I have never succeeded in writing a bestseller. And now I know why. I can't cook.

Had I been able to do so, I could have turned out a few of those sumptuous looking cookery books that brighten up the bookstore windows before being snapped up by folk who can't cook either.

As it is, if I were forced to write a cook book, it would probably be called *Fifty Different Ways of Boiling An Egg*, and other disasters.

I used to think that boiling an egg would be a simple undertaking. But when I came to live at 7,000 ft in the Himalayan foothills, I found that just getting the water to boil was something of an achievement. I don't know if it's the altitude or the density of the water, but it just won't come to a boil in time for breakfast. As a result my eggs are only half-boiled. 'Never mind,' I tell everyone; 'half-boiled eggs are more nutritious than full-boiled eggs.'

'Why boil them at all?' asks my five-year old grandson, Gautam, who is my Mr Dick, always offering good advice. 'Raw eggs are probably healthier.'

'Just you wait and see,' I told him. 'I'll make you a cheese omelette you'll never forget.' And I did. It was a bit messy, as I was over-generous with the tomatoes, but I thought it tasted rather good. Gautam, however, pushed his plate away, saying, 'You forgot to put in the egg.'

101 Failed Omelettes might well be the title of my bestseller.

I love watching other people cook—a habit that I acquired at a young age, when I would watch my Granny at work in the kitchen, turning out delicious curries, koftas and custards. I would try helping her, but she soon put a stop to my feeble contributions. On one occasion she asked me to add a cup of spices to a large curry dish she was preparing, and absent-mindedly I added a cup of sugar. The result—a very sweet curry! Another invention of mine.

I was better at remembering Granny's kitchen proverbs. Here are some of them:

'There is skill in all things, even in making porridge.'

'Dry bread at home is better then curried prawns abroad.'

'Eating and drinking should not keep men from thinking.'

'Better a small fish than an empty dish.'

And her favourite maxim, with which she reprimanded me

whenever I showed signs of gluttony: 'Don't let your tongue cut your throat.'

And as for making porridge, it's certainly no simple matter. I made one or two attempts, but it always came out lumpy.

'What's this?' asked Gautam suspiciously, when I offered him some.

'Porridge!' I said enthusiastically. 'It's eaten by those brave Scottish Highlanders who were always fighting the English!'

'And did they win?' he asked.

'Well—er—not usually. But they were outnumbered!'

He looked doubtfully at the porridge. 'Some other time,' he said.

So why not take the advice of Thoreau and try to simplify life? Simplify, simplify! Or simply sandwiches...

These shouldn't be too difficult, I decided. After all, they are basically bread and butter. But have you tried cutting bread into thin slices? Don't. It's highly dangerous. If you're a pianist, you could be putting your career at great risk.

You must get your bread ready sliced. Butter it generously. Now add your fillings. Cheese, tomato, lettuce, cucumber, whatever. Gosh, I was really going places! Slap another slice of buttered bread over this mouth-watering assemblage. Now cut in two. Result: Everything spills out at the sides and on to the table-cloth.

'Now look what you've gone and done,' says Gautam, in his best Oliver Hardy manner.

'Never mind,' I tell him. 'Practice makes perfect!'

And one of these days you're going to find *Bond's Book of Better Sandwiches* up there on the bestseller lists.

From the Primaeval Past

I discovered the pool near Rajpur on a hot summer's day, some fifteen years ago. It was shaded by close-growing Sal trees, and looked cool and inviting. I took off my clothes and dived in.

The water was colder than I had expected. It was icy, glacial cold. The sun never touched it for long, I supposed. Striking out vigorously, I swam to the other end of the pool and pulled myself up on the rocks, shivering.

But I wanted to swim. So I dived in again and did a gentle breast-stroke towards the middle of the pool. Something slid between my legs. Something slimy, pulpy. I could see no one, hear nothing. I swam away, but the floating, slippery thing followed me. I did not like it. Something curled around my leg. Not an underwater plant. Something that sucked at my foot. A long tongue licking at my calf. I struck out wildly, thrust myself away from whatever it was that sought my company. Something lonely, lurking in the shadows. Kicking up spray, I swam like a frightened porpoise fleeing from some terror of the deep.

Safely out of the water, I looked for a warm, sunny rock, and stood there looking down at the water.

Nothing stirred. The surface of the pool was now calm and undisturbed. Just a few fallen leaves floating around. Not a frog, not a fish, not a water-bird in sight. And that in itself seemed strange, for you would have expected some sort of pond life to have been in evidence.

But something lived in the pool, of that I was sure. Something very cold-blooded; colder and wetter than the water. Could it have been a corpse trapped in the weeds? I did not want to know; so I dressed and hurried away.

A few days later I left for Delhi, where I went to work in an ad agency, telling people how to beat the summer heat by drinking fizzy drinks that made you thirstier. The pool in the forest was forgotten. And it was ten years before I visited Rajpur again.

Leaving the small hotel where I was staying, I found myself walking through the same old Sal forest, drawn almost irresistibly towards the pool where I had not been able to finish my swim. I was not over-eager to swim there again, but I was curious to know if the pool still existed.

Well, it was there all right, although the surroundings had changed and a number of new houses and buildings had come up where formerly there had only been wilderness. And there was a fair amount of activity in the vicinity of the pool.

A number of labourers were busy with buckets and rubber pipes, doing their best to empty the pool. They had also dammed off and diverted the little stream that fed it.

Overseeing this operation was a well-dressed man in a white safari suit. I thought at first that he was an honorary forest warden, but it turned out that he was the owner of a new school that had come up nearby.

'Do you live in Rajpur?' he asked.

'I used to ... once upon a time ... Why are you draining the pool?'

'It's become a hazard,' he said. 'Two of my boys were drowned here recently. Both senior students. Of course they weren't supposed to be swimming here without permission, the pool is off limits. But you know what boys are like. Make a rule and they feel duty-bound to break it.'

He told me his name, Kapoor, and led me back to his house, a newly-built bungalow with a wide cool verandah. His servant brought us glasses of cool sherbet. We sat in cane chairs overlooking the pool and the forest. Across a clearing, a gravelled road led to the school buildings, newly white-washed and glistening in the sun.

'Were the boys there at the same time?' I asked.

'Yes, they were friends. And they must have been attacked by fiends. Limbs twisted and broken, faces disfigured. But death was due to drowning—that was the verdict of the medical examiner.'

We gazed down at the shallows of the pool, where a couple of men were still at work, the others having gone for their mid-day meal.

'Perhaps it would be better to leave the place alone,' I said. 'Put a barbed-wire fence around it. Keep your boys away. Thousands of years ago this valley was an inland sea. A few small pools and streams are all that is left of it.'

'I want to fill it in and build something there. An open-air theatre, maybe. We can always create an artificial pond somewhere else.'

Presently only one man remained at the pool, knee-deep in muddy, churned-up water. And Mr Kapoor and I both saw what happened next.

Something rose out of the bottom of the pool. It looked like a giant snail, but its head was part human, its body and limbs part squid or octopus. An enormous succubus. It stood taller than the man in the pool. A creature soft and slimy, a survivor from our primaeval past.

With a great sucking motion it enveloped the man completely, so that only his arms and legs could be seen thrashing about wildly and futilely. The succubus dragged him down under the water.

Kapoor and I left the verandah and ran to the edge of the pool. Bubbles rose from the green scum near the surface. All was still and silent. And then, like bubble-gum issuing from the mouth of a child, the mangled body of the man shot out of the water and came spinning towards us.

Dead and drowned and sucked dry of its fluids.

Naturally no more work was done at the pool. A labourer had slipped and fallen to his death on the rocks, that was the story that was put out. Kapoor swore me to secrecy. His school would have to close down if there were too many strange drownings and accidents in its vicinity. But he walled the place off from his property and made it practically inaccessible. The jungle's undergrowth now hides the approach.

The monsoon rains came and the pool filled up again. I can tell you how to get there, if you'd like to see it. But I wouldn't advise you to go for a swim.

In a Crystal Ball: A Mussoorie Mystery

Conan Doyle, the creator of Sherlock Holmes, had a lifelong interest in unusual criminal cases, and his friends often passed on to him interesting accounts of crime and detection from around the world. It was in this way that he learnt of the strange death of Miss Frances Garnett-Orme in the Indian hill-station of Mussoorie. Here was a murder combining the weird borders of the occult with a crime mystery as inexplicable as any devised by Doyle himself.

In April 1912 (shortly before the Titanic went down) Conan Doyle received a letter from his Sussex neighbour Rudyard Kipling:

> *Dear Doyle,*
> *There has been a murder in India. ... A murder by suggestion at Mussoorie, which is one of the most curious things in its line on record.*

Everything that is improbable and on the face of it impossible is in this case.

Kipling had received details of the case from a friend working in the Allahabad *Pioneer*, a paper for which, as a young man, he had worked in the 1880s. Urging Doyle to pursue the story, Kipling concluded: 'The psychology alone is beyond description.'

Doyle was indeed interested to hear more, for India had furnished him with material in the past, as in *The Sign of Four* and several short stories. Kipling, too, had turned to crime and detection in his early stories of Strickland of the Indian Police. The two writers got together and discussed the case, which was indeed a fascinating affair.

The scene was set in Mussoorie, a popular hill-station in the foothills of the Himalayas. It wasn't as grand as Simla (where the Viceroy and his entourage went) but it was a charming and convivial place, with a number of hotels and boarding-houses, a small military cantonment, and several private schools for European children.

It was during the summer 'season' of 1911 that Miss Frances Garnett-Orme came to stay in Mussoorie, taking a suite at the Savoy, a popular resort hotel. On 28 July she celebrated her 49th birthday. She was the daughter of George Garnett-Orme, of Skipton-in-Craven in Yorkshire, a district registrar of the Country Court. It was a family important enough to be counted among the landed gentry. Her father had died in 1892.

She came out to India in 1893 with the intention of marrying Jack Grant of the United Provinces Police. But he died in 1894 and she went back to England. Upset by his death following so soon after her father's, she turned to spiritualism in the hope of communicating with him. We must remember that spiritualism was all the rage in the early years of the century, seances and table-rappings being part of the social scene both in England and India. Madam Blavatsky, the chief exponent of spiritualism, was probably at the height of her popularity around this time; she spent her 'seasons' in neighbouring Simla, where she had many followers.

Miss Garnett-Orme's life was unsettled. She was drawn back to India, returning in 1901 to live in Lucknow, the regional capital of the United Provinces. She was still in contact with Jack Grant's family and saw his brother occasionally. The summer of 1907 was spent at Naini Tal, a hill-station popular with Lucknow residents. It was here that she met Miss Eva Mountstephen, who was working as a governess.

Eva Mountstephen, too, had an interest in spiritualism. It appears that she had actually told several of her friends about this time that she had learnt (in the course of a seancé) that in 1911 she would come into a great deal of money.

We are told that there was something sinister about Miss Mountstephen. She specialised in crystal-gazing, and what she saw in the glass often took a violent form. Her 'control', that is her connection in the spirit world, was a dead friend named Mrs Winter.

As a result of their common interest in the occult, Miss Garnett-Orme took on the younger woman as a companion when she returned to Lucknow in the winter. There they settled down together. But the summers were spent at one of the various hill-stations. Was there a latent lesbianism in their relationship? It was a restless, rootless life, but they were held together by the strong and heady influence of the seancé table and the crystal ball. Miss Garnett-Orme's indifferent health also made her dependent on the younger woman.

In the summer of 1911, the couple went up to Mussoorie, probably the most frivolous of hill-stations, where 'seasonal' love affairs were almost the order of the day. They took rooms in the Savoy. Electricity had yet to reach Mussoorie, and it was still the age of candelabras and gas-lit streets. Every house had a grand piano. If you didn't go out to a ball, you sang or danced at home. But Miss Garnett-Orme's spiritual pursuits took precedence over these more mundane entertainments. Towards the end of the 'season', on 12 September, Miss Mountstephen returned to Lucknow to pack up their household for a move to Jhansi, where they planned to spend the winter.

On the morning of 19 September, while Miss Mountstephen was still away, Miss Garnett-Orme was found dead in her bed. The door was locked from the inside. On her bedside table was a glass. She was positioned on the bed as though laid out by a nurse or undertaker.

Because of these puzzling circumstances, Major Birdwood of the Indian Medical Service (who was the Civil Surgeon in Mussoorie) was called in. He decided to hold an autopsy. It was discovered that Miss Garnett-Orme had been poisoned with prussic acid.

Prussic acid is a quick-acting poison, and would have killed too quickly for the victim to have composed herself in the way she was found. An ayah told the police that she had seen someone (she could not tell whether it was a man or a woman) slipping away through a large skylight and escaping over the roof.

Hill-stations are hot-beds of rumour and intrigue, and of course the gossips had a field day. Miss Garnett-Orme suffered from dyspepsia and was always dosing herself from a large bottle of Sodium Bicarbonate, which was regularly refilled. It was alleged that the bottle had been tampered with, that an unknown white powder had been added. Her doctor was questioned thoroughly. They even questioned a touring mind-reader, Mr Alfred Capper, who claimed that Miss Mountstephen had hurried from a room rather than have her mind read!

After several weeks the police arrested Miss Mountstephen. Although she had a convincing alibi (due to her absence in Jhansi) the police sought to prove that some kind of sinister influence had been exerted on Miss Garnett-Orme to take her medicine at a particular time. Thus, through suggestion, the murderer could kill and yet be away at the time of death. In her first novel, *The Mysterious Affair at Styles* (1920), the poisoner was in a distant place by the time her victim reached the fatal dose, the poison having precipitated to the bottom of the mixture. Perhaps Miss Christie read accounts of the Garnett-Orme case in the British press. Even the motive was similar.

But there was no Hercule Poirot in Mussoorie, and in court this theory could never be made convincing. The police case was never strong (they would have done better to have followed the ayah's lead), and it appears that they only acted because there was considerable ill-feeling in Mussoorie against Miss Mountstephen.

When the trial came up at Allahabad in March 1912, it caused a sensation. Murder by remote-control was something new in the annals of crime. But after hearing many days of evidence about the ladies' way of life, about crystal-gazing and premonitions of death, the court found Miss Mountstephen innocent. The Chief Justice, in delivering his verdict, remarked that the true circumstances of Miss Garnett-Orme's death would probably never be known. And he was right.

Miss Mountstephen applied for probate of her friend's will. But the Garnett-Orme family in England sent out her brother, Mr Hunter Garnett-Orme, to contest it. The case went in favour of Mr Garnett-Orme. The District Judge (W.D. Burkitt) turned down Miss Mountstephen's application on grounds of 'fraud and undue influence in connection with spiritualism and crystal gazing'. She went in appeal to the Allahabad High Court, but the Lower Court's decision was upheld.

Miss Mountstephen returned to England. We do not know her state of mind, but if she was innocent, she must have been a deeply embittered woman. Miss Garnett-Orme's doctor lost his flourishing practice in Mussoorie and left the country too. There were rumours that he and Miss Mountstephen had conspired to get hold of Miss Garnett-Orme's considerable fortune.

There was one more puzzling feature of the case. Mr Charles Jackson, a painter friend of many of those involved, had died suddenly, apparently of cholera, two months after Miss Garnett-Orme's mysterious death. The police took an interest in his sudden demise. When he was exhumed on 23 December, the body was found to be in a perfect state of preservation. He had died of arsenic poisoning.

Murder or suicide? This puzzle, too, was never resolved. Was there a connection with Miss Garnett-Orme's death? That too we shall never know. Had Conan Doyle taken up Kipling's suggestion and involved himself in the case (as he had done in so many others in England), perhaps the outcome would have been different.

As it is, we can only make our own conjectures.

A Job Well Done

Dhuki, the gardener, was clearing up the weeds that grew in profusion around the old disused well. He was an old man, skinny and bent and spindly-legged; but he had always been like that; his strength lay in his wrists and in his long, tendril-like fingers. He looked as frail as a petunia, but he had the tenacity of a vine.

'Are you going to cover the well?' I asked. I was eight, a great favourite of Dhuki. He had been the gardener long before my birth; had worked for my father, until my father died, and now worked for my mother and stepfather.

'I must cover it, I suppose,' said Dhuki. 'That's what the "Major sahib" wants. He'll be back any day, and if he finds the well still uncovered, he'll get into one of his raging fits and I'll be looking for another job!'

The 'Major sahib' was my stepfather, Major Summerskill. A tall, hearty, back-slapping man, who liked polo and pig-sticking. He was quite unlike my father. My father had always given me books to read. The Major said I would become a dreamer if I read too much, and took the books away. I hated him and did not think much of my mother for marrying him.

'The boy's too soft,' I heard him tell my mother. 'I must see that he gets riding lessons.'

But before the riding lessons could be arranged, the Major's regiment was ordered to Peshawar. Trouble was expected from some of the frontier tribes. He was away for about two months. Before leaving, he had left strict instructions for Dhuki to cover up the old well.

'Too damned dangerous having an open well in the middle of the garden,' my stepfather had said. 'Make sure that it's completely covered by the time I get back.'

Dhuki was loath to cover up the old well. It had been there for over fifty years, long before the house had been built. In its walls lived a colony of pigeons. Their soft cooing filled the garden with a lovely sound. And during the hot, dry, summer months, when taps ran dry, the well was always a dependable source of water. The bhisti still used it, filling his goatskin bag with the cool clear water and sprinkling the paths around the house to keep the dust down.

Dhuki pleaded with my mother to let him leave the well uncovered.

'What will happen to the pigeons?' he asked.

'Oh, surely they can find another well,' said my mother. 'Do close it up soon, Dhuki. I don't want the Sahib to come back and find that you haven't done anything about it.'

My mother seemed just a little bit afraid of the Major. How can we be afraid of those we love? It was a question that puzzled me then, and puzzles me still.

The Major's absence made life pleasant again. I returned to my books, spent long hours in my favourite banyan tree, ate buckets of mangoes, and dawdled in the garden talking to Dhuki.

Neither he nor I were looking forward to the Major's return. Dhuki had stayed on after my mother's second marriage only out of loyalty to her and affection for me; he had really been my father's man. But my mother had always appeared deceptively frail and helpless, and most men, Major Summerskill included, felt protective towards her. She liked people who did things for her.

'Your father liked this well,' said Dhuki. 'He would often sit here in the evenings, with a book in which he made drawings of birds and flowers and insects.'

I remembered those drawings, and I remembered how they had all been thrown away by the Major when he had moved into the house. Dhuki knew about it, too. I didn't keep much from him.

'It's a sad business closing this well,' said Dhuki again. 'Only a fool or a drunkard is likely to fall into it.'

But he had made his preparations. Planks of sal wood, bricks and cement were neatly piled up around the well.

'Tomorrow,' said Dhuki. 'Tomorrow I will do it. Not today. Let the birds remain for one more day. In the morning, Baba, you can help me drive the birds from the well.

On the day my stepfather was expected back, my mother hired a tonga and went to the bazaar to do some shopping. Only a few people had cars in those days. Even colonels went about in tongas. Now, a clerk finds it beneath his dignity to sit in one.

As the Major was not expected before evening, I decided I would make full use of my last free morning. I took all my favourite books and stored them away in an outhouse where I could come for them from time to time. Then, my pockets bursting with mangoes, I climbed into the banyan tree. It was the darkest and coolest place on a hot day in June.

From behind the screen of leaves that concealed me, I could see Dhuki moving about near the well. He appeared to be most unwilling to get on with the job of covering it up.

'Baba!' he called, several times; but I did not feel like stirring from the banyan tree. Dhuki grasped a long plank of wood and placed it across one end of the well. He started hammering. From my vantage point in the banyan tree, he looked very bent and old.

A jingle of tonga bells and the squeak of unoiled wheels told me that a tonga was coming in at the gate. It was too early for my mother to be back. I peered through the thick, waxy leaves of the tree, and nearly fell off my branch in surprise. It was my stepfather, the Major! He had arrived earlier than expected.

I did not come down from the tree. I had no intention of confronting my stepfather until my mother returned.

The Major had climbed down from the tonga and was watching his luggage being carried on to the verandah. He was red in the face and the ends of his handlebar moustache were stiff with brilliantine. Dhuki approached with a half-hearted salaam.

'Ah, so there you are, you old scoundrel!' exclaimed the Major, trying to sound friendly and jocular. 'More jungle than garden, from what I can see. You're getting too old for this sort of work, Dhuki. Time to retire! And where's the Memsahib?'

'Gone to the bazaar,' said Dhuki.

'And the boy?'

Dhuki shrugged. 'I have not seen the boy, today, Sahib.'

'Damn!' said the Major. 'A fine homecoming, this is. Well, wake up the cook-boy and tell him to get some sodas.'

'Cook-boy's gone away,' said Dhuki.

'Well, I'll be double-damned,' said the major.

The tonga went away, and the Major started pacing up and down the garden path. Then he saw Dhuki's unfinished work at the well. He grew purple in the face, strode across to the well, and started ranting at the old gardener.

Dhuki began making excuses. He said something about a shortage of bricks; the sickness of a niece; unsatisfactory cement; unfavourable weather; unfavourable gods. When none of this seemed to satisfy the Major, Dhuki began mumbling about something bubbling up from the bottom of the well, and pointed down into its depths. The Major stepped on to the low parapet and looked down. Dhuki kept pointing. The Major leant over a little.

Dhuki's hands moved swiftly, like a conjurer's making a pass. He did not actually push the Major. He appeared merely to tap him once on the bottom. I caught a glimpse of my stepfather's boots as he disappeared into the well. I couldn't help thinking of Alice in Wonderland, of Alice disappearing down the rabbit hole.

There was a tremendous splash, and the pigeons flew up, circling the well thrice before settling on the roof of the bungalow.

By lunch time—or tiffin, as we called it then—Dhuki had the well covered over with the wooden planks.

'The Major will be pleased,' said my mother, when she came home. 'It will be quite ready by evening, won't it, Dhuki?'

By evening, the well had been completely bricked over. It was the fastest bit of work Dhuki had ever done.

Over the next few weeks, my mother's concern changed to anxiety, her anxiety to melancholy, and her melancholy to resignation. By being gay and high-spirited myself, I hope I did something to cheer her up. She had written to the Colonel of the Regiment, and had been informed that the Major had gone home on leave a fortnight previously. Somewhere, in the vastness of India, the Major had disappeared.

It was easy enough to disappear and never be found. After several months had passed without the Major turning up, it was presumed that one of the two things must have happened. Either he had been murdered on the train, and his corpse flung into a river; or, he had run away with a tribal girl and was living in some remote corner of the country.

Life had to carry on for the rest of us. The rains were over, and the guava season was approaching.

My mother was receiving visits from a colonel of His Majesty's 32nd Foot. He was an elderly, easy-going, seemingly absent-minded man, who didn't get in the way at all, but left slabs of chocolate lying around the house.

'A *good* Sahib,' observed Dhuki, as I stood beside him behind the bougainvillaea, watching the colonel saunter up the verandah steps. 'See how well he wears his sola-topee! It covers his head completely.'

'He's bald underneath,' I said.

'No matter. I think he will be all right.'

'And if he isn't,' I said, 'we can always open up the well again.'

Dhuki dropped the nozzle of the hosepipe, and water gushed out over our feet. But he recovered quickly, and taking me by the hand, led me across to the old well, now surmounted by a three-tiered cement platform which looked rather like a wedding cake.

'We must not forget our old well,' he said. 'Let us make it beautiful, Baba. Some flower pots, perhaps.'

And together we fetched pots, and decorated the covered well with ferns and geraniums. Everyone congratulated Dhuki on the fine job he'd done. My only regret was that the pigeons had gone away.

The Earthquake

'If ever there's a calamity,' Grandmother used to say, 'it will find Grandfather in his bath.' Grandfather loved his bath—which he took in a large round aluminum tub—and sometimes spent as long as an hour in it, 'wallowing' as he called it, and splashing around like a boy.

He was in his bath during the earthquake that convulsed Bengal and Assam on 12 June 1897—an earthquake so severe that even today the region of the great Brahmaputra river basin hasn't settled down. Not long ago it was reported that the entire Shillong Plateau had moved an appreciable distance away from the Geological Survey of India; this shift has been taking place gradually over the past eighty years.

Had Grandfather been alive, he would have added one more clipping to his scrapbook on earthquakes. The clipping goes in anyway, because the scrapbook is now with his children. More than newspaper accounts of the disaster, it was Grandfather's own letters and memoirs that made the earthquake seem recent and vivid; for he, along with Grandmother and two of their children (one of them my father), was living in Shillong, a picturesque little hill-station in Assam, when the earth shook and the mountains heaved.

As I have mentioned, Grandfather was in his bath, splashing about, and did not hear the first rumbling. But Grandmother was in the garden hanging out or taking in the washing (she could never remember which) when, suddenly, the animals began making a hideous noise—a sure intimation of a natural disaster, for animals sense the approach of an earthquake much more quickly than humans.

The crows all took wing, wheeling wildly overhead and cawing loudly. The chickens flapped in circles, as if they were being chased. Two dogs sitting on the verandah suddenly jumped up and ran out with their tails between their legs. Within half a minute of her noticing the noise made by the animals, Grandmother heard a rattling, rumbling noise, like the approach of a train.

The noise increased for about a minute, and then there was the first trembling of the ground. The animals by this time all seemed to have gone mad. Treetops lashed backwards and forwards, doors banged and windows shook, and Grandmother swore later that the house actually swayed in front of her. She had difficulty in standing straight, though this could have been more due to the trembling of her knees than to the trembling of the ground.

The first shock lasted for about a minute and a half. 'I was in my tub having a bath,' Grandfather wrote for posterity, 'which for the first time in the last two months I had taken in the afternoon instead of in the morning. My wife and children and the maid were downstairs. Then the shock came and a quaking, which increased in intensity every second. It was like putting so many shells in a basket, and shaking them up with a rapid sifting motion from side to side.

'At first I did not realise what it was that caused my tub to sway about and the water to splash. I rose up, and found the earth heaving, while the washstand basin, ewer, cups and glasses danced and rocked about in the most hideous fashion. I rushed to the inner door to open it and search for my wife and children but could not move the dratted door as boxes, furniture and plaster had come up against it. The back door was the only way of escape. I managed to open, and, thank god, was able to get out. All the sections of the thatched roof had slithered down on the four sides like a pack of cards and blocked all the exits and entrances.

'With only a towel wrapped around my waist, I ran into the open to the front of the house, but found only my wife there. The whole front of the house was blocked by the fallen section of thatch from the roof. Through this I broke my way under the iron railings and extricated the others. The bearer had pluckily borne the weight of the whole thatched roof section on his back, and in this way saved the maid and children from being crushed beneath it.'

After the main shock of the earthquake had passed, minor shocks took place at regular intervals of five minutes or so, all through the night. But during that first shakeup, the town of Shillong was reduced to ruin and rubble. Everything made of masonry was brought to the ground. Government House, the post office, the jail, all tumbled down. When the jail fell, the prisoners, instead of making their escape, sat huddled on the road waiting for the superintendent to come to their aid.

'The ground began to heave and shake,' wrote a young girl in a newspaper called *The Englishman*. 'I stayed on my bicycle for a second, and then fell off and got up and tried to run, staggering about from side to side of the road. To my left I saw great clouds of dust, which I afterwards discovered to be houses falling and the earth slipping from the sides of the hills. To my right I saw the small dam at the end of the lake torn asunder and the water rushing out, the wooden bridge across the lake break in two and the sides of the lake falling in; and at my feet the ground cracking and opening. I was wild with fear and didn't know which way to turn.'

The lake rose up like a mountain, and then totally disappeared, leaving only a swamp of red mud. Not a house was left standing. People were rushing about, wives looking for husbands, parents looking for children, not knowing whether their loved ones were alive or dead. A crowd of people had collected on the cricket ground, which was considered the safest place; but Grandfather and the family took shelter in a small shop on the road outside his house. The shop was a rickety wooden structure, which had always looked as though it would fall down in a strong wind. But it withstood the earthquake.

And then the rain came and it poured. This was extraordinary, because before the earthquake there wasn't a cloud to be seen; but five minutes after, the shock was felt for more than a hundred miles on the Assam-Bengal Railway. A train overturned at Shamshernagar; another was derailed at Mantolla. Over a thousand people lost lives in the Cherrapunji Hills, and in other areas, too, the death toll was heavy.

The Brahmaputra burst its banks and many cultivators were drowned in the flood. A tiger was found drowned. And in North Bhagalpur, where the earthquake started, two elephants sat down in the bazaar and refused to get up until the following morning.

Over a hundred men, who were at work in Shillong's Government printing press, were caught in the building when it collapsed, and though the men of Gurkha regiment did splendid rescue work, only a few were brought out alive. One of those killed in Shillong was Mr McCabe, a British official. Grandfather described the ruins of Mr McCabe's house: 'Here a bedpost, there a sword, a broken desk or chair, a bit of torn carpet, a well-known hat with its Indian Civil Service colours, battered books, speaking reminiscenes of the man we mourn,'

While most houses collapsed where they stood, Government House, it seems, fell backwards. The church was a mass of red stones in an ugly disorder. The organ was a tortured wreck.

A few days later the family, with other refugees, were making their way to Calcutta to stay with friends or relatives. It was a slow, tedious journey, with many interruptions, for the roads and railway lines had been badly damaged, and passengers had often to be transported in trolleys. Grandfather was rather struck at the stoicism displayed by an assistant engineer. At one station a telegram was handed to the engineer informing him that his bungalow had been destroyed. 'Beastly nuisance,' he observed with an aggrieved air. 'I've seen it cave in during a storm, but this is the first time it has played me such a trick on account of an earthquake.'

The family got to Calcutta to find the inhabitants of the capital in a panic; for they too had felt the quake and were expecting it to recur. The damage in Calcutta was slight compared to the devastation elsewhere, but nerves were on the edge, and people slept in the open or in carriages. Cracks and fissures had appeared in a number of old buildings, and Grandfather was among the many who were worried at the proposal to fire a salute of sixty guns on Jubilee Day (the Diamond Jubilee of Queen Victoria). They felt the gunfire would bring down a number of shaky buildings. Obviously Grandfather did not wish to be caught in his bath a second time. However, Queen Victoria was not to be deprived of her salute. The guns were duly fired, and Calcutta remained standing.

The Demon Driver

At driving a car I've never been good—
I batter the bumper and damage the hood—
'Get off the road!' the traffic cops shout,
'You're supposed to go *round* that roundabout!'
'I thought it was quicker to drive straight through.'
'Give us your license — it's time to renew.'
I took their advice and handed a fee
To a Babu who looked on this windfall with glee.
'No problem,' he said, 'Your license now pukka,
You may drive all the way from here to Kolkata.'

So away I drove, at a feverish pitch,
Advancing someway down an unseen ditch.
Once back on the highway, I soon joined the fray
Of hundreds of drivers who wouldn't give way:
I skimmed past a truck and revolved round a van
(Good drivers can do anything that they can)
Then offered a lift to a man with a load—

'Just a little way down to the end of this road,'
As I pressed on the pedal, the car gave a shudder:
He'd got in at one door, got out at the other.
'God help you!' he said, as he hurried away,
'I'll come for a drive another fine day!'
I came to that roundabout, round it I sped
Eager to get to my dinner and bed.
Round it I went, and round it once more
'Get off the road!' That cop was a bore.
I swung to the left and went clean through a wall,
My neighbour stood there — he looked menacing, tall—
'This will cost you three thousand,' he quietly said,
'And send me your cheque before you're in bed!'

Alas! my new car was sent for repair,
But my friends gathered round and said, never despair!
'We are all going to help you to make a fresh start.'
And next day they gave me a nice bullock-cart.